black men vs White Men

the Black Woman's Choice

Written by: Cicely J and Marlon Green

CRJ Publishing

DEDICATIONS

This book is dedicated to all the good black men out there who still love and are attracted to good black women. This is for all the fathers out there who take an active part in their children's lives even if they are not with the mother. This book is dedicated to you Daddy! May your soul always rest in peace in knowing that you did an awesome job and I will always love you.

Ces

CRJ Publishing, LLC

Copyright © 2011 by CRJ PUBLISHING, LLC
CRJ Publishing, LLC
6664 Sawgrass Lane
Vallejo, CA 94591

Library of Congress Cataloging – in – Publication Data is available.

ISBN-13: 978-0-615-320939 (Pbk)

Registered with the IP Rights Office
Copyright Registration Service
Ref: 1863610958

CICELY J'S ACKNOWLEDGMENTS

I cannot promote anything I have done without taking the time to appreciate and thank the people who have had so much of an impact on my life. So many people start off speeches thanking God because they think it is the proper thing to do. I don't just thank Him for my success, I thank him for my life! I thank Him for giving me the tools to do exactly what I have always wanted to do and for giving me the mind to be able to execute my ideas and make my dreams a reality. I have a relationship with God, and my Lord and Savior Jesus Christ. I don't just thank Him when I win an award or write something. I praise and thank Him every day.

In Loving Memory:
To my father, Pastor Ronald J Johnson, Sr. who did not live to see this day, but prophesied this day to me when I was a teenager. My father always told me I would do great things and achieve even more than he did. My father was a great man and I miss him dearly but I know he is looking over me proud that his little girl did it! I love you Daddy. You are the wind beneath my wings.

My maternal grandfather Alfonso Brown aka "Papa". Whenever I had to write about my hero during Black History Month I always chose to write about Papa. My cousins did too. He was truly a powerful black man. At 6'4 he was so gentle and so wise and I remember the days we shared watching tv in his den talking about the World War II. He loved his grandkids. He would have been proud to tears if he was with us. I love you Papa!

My paternal grandmother Christine Johnson aka Grandmama. She was a little ball of fire at 4'10. Grandmama was so sweet and so beautiful and she prayed for her grandchildren every night before she went to bed. I am so glad that the "prayers of the righteous availeth much." I am sure she and my dad are sharing a pecan pie in heaven right now. I love you Grandmama!

To my long time family friend Kenny Tyson. Kenny encouraged me to go for it when no one else did. He loved my parents so much and he wanted to invest in me and my project. We talked about it a few times and I was finally ready to show him what I was working on. We were going to set a date to meet so he could see my manuscript and he passed away just weeks before we were going to meet. I love Kenny and the entire Tyson family. Kenny I did it!

To my pastor Danny Jefferson for letting me be me and not judging me for it. You understand my uniqueness and accept me how I am. I appreciate that. You keeps it real. To my entire church family at Rehoboth World Outreach Center COGIC, y'all know the real me and I feel so loved and missed when I am away from home.

I have only 3 biological siblings and I love them dearly. Angela for being my mom when ours was working too hard, Ronnie Jr. for teaching me about "the boys" and protecting me from myself, and Rhachelle for just being Rhachelle. I have several surrogate sisters and brothers who have made my life full and phenomenal. Alana (my BFF 4 life!), Davia, Andrea, Rachelle, Lorraine, DeDe, and Jill. The fellas, Alonzo, Donnie, Paul, Berwyn, Gamon, and Groux. You all are my family and I love you to life!

My friends/family Kevin and Rita. You two I can't even explain. It's just love. That's all I can say. Get Benicia and meet me at Happy Hour! Lonnie aka St Louis, your words of encouragement helps me keep pushing. You came up! LOL.
My cousins Lisa and Nicole who are my road dawgs. We are an extremely close family and since Angela and Rhachelle moved

to Vegas, you have been my sisters. To my cousins April and Alana for being the epitome of success for black women. I am proud to be your blood.

To my aunts whom I love so so very much. Auntie Freda you are my homie. I love you so much. You are not just my aunt, I consider you my friend. Auntie Paulette, my uncle hit the jackpot when he married you. I want to be like you when I grow up. You have been such a wonderful example for me to follow. Aunt Yvonne, Auntie Bettye, and Aunt Ann thank you for loving me unconditionally.

My Uncle Mike for always being a solid voice of reason. You remind me of my dad and I appreciate your sound advice. Uncle Sargent and Uncle Curtis, my dad's two brothers whom he loved so much. Thank you for holding me up when my World was turned upside down.

My grandfather Sargent Johnson, Sr. Papa has been an entrepreneur since before I was born. I guess that's why I have always found it hard having to punch the clock. Working for myself is in my DNA. I love you Papa Johnson.

My grandmother who we call Bigmama. She loves all of us the same (I think), and most of the time she never shows favorites. She is the peach cobbler making, homemade mac and cheese, fresh greens from the garden type of grandma. I miss your cooking but you sure know how to direct traffic in the kitchen from your lounge chair in the den. Gotta love Bigmama.

My mom, the diva, the "I shoulda been a model in the 60s" grandmother of 13 who wears a size 8. Missionary Rachel Queen Ester Johnson who is called Ms. Q' in her world. Thank you for being so hard on me and never letting me bring home a C. I thought you were the meanest, strictest, most stern mother ever!

For years I secretly called you Mommy Dearest. I love you, I appreciate you, and thank you! It made me who I am today.

To the most important person to me on this entire planet, my son, LJ. Thank you for being so mature and sharing your mommy with the world. You are the type of child every parent dreams of. You make your dad and I proud every day. Thank you Jon for being such a good father and allowing me to be able to do what I do. You two are a gift.

To my co-author Marlon for assisting me with this project when I didn't even know exactly what direction I wanted to go in. You were so patient with me. Thank you for your professionalism and guidance. To my family at Dreams Publications, Dr. Linda Hodo and Eddie Robinson for encouraging my dream and watching my manuscript become a published work.

My confidante, brother, adviser, unofficial manager, bodyguard, one of my closest friends, Jabari Ali. Over the past 6 or more years you have been in my corner advising me on what should be my next move. I finally listened! Thank you for everything.

To my publicist Fran Briggs, for taking the thoughts out of my head and putting them in print. Books don't leave the shelf without good PR. Thank you for being so good at what you do.

To my editor Joan Adrian. You took my words and gave them life! For that I am eternally grateful.

To everyone I didn't mention because of space, I love you lots. I want to put Vallejo on the map so we can do it big! I love all my family and I love all my friends. Keep me in your daily prayers.

Peace.
Cicely J

MARLON GREEN'S ACKNOWLEDGMENTS

I sincerely thank my brilliant mother and my aunts for always being the smartest, sharpest, and classiest women on the planet. Thank you for always providing me with the hope of what I could find in a woman.

Special thanks to Cicely J for allowing me to join her in this journey. May this book take you places beyond your dreams. It's amazing how we met and what transpired that day. The result is the debate encompassed within these pages. I'm really happy that your time has finally arrived.

And to all of the intelligent, beautiful, sweet, passionate, adorable Black women that supply my soul with the essentials, thank you for your guidance, your love, your energy, and your influence. Without you, I'd be lost.

Marlon Green

TABLE OF CONTENTS

PREFACE

Does Life Imitate TV or Does TV Imitate Life?
Why Black Women Can't Seem to Find Eligible black men
Black Women and White Men: What Is Really Going On?

CHAPTER 1 Black Men in Jail vs.Black Men in College   21
           Prison Population exceeds Two Million

CHAPTER 2 Black Men and Commitments   25

CHAPTER 3 How Does a Black Woman Raise a   32
           Black Man Alone?
           Classic Baby Mama Syndrome

CHAPTER 4 Black Men Are Not Faithful!   43

CHAPTER 5 Black Men Want to be Taken Care Of   52

CHAPTER 6 Black Men Have Given Up on Black Women   62
           Will the Real Women Please Stand Up!

CHAPTER 7 Black Men Don't Know What They Want   66

CHAPTER 8 Black Men Mature Ten Years Behind   74
           Everyone Else

CHAPTER 9   Successful Black Men Want White or   80
Latina Women

CHAPTER 10   Black Men on the 'DL'   84

CHAPTER 11   Lipstick Lesbians   87

CHAPTER 12   The Exception to the Rule   90

CHAPTER 13   Blame It on the Rain   100

CHAPTER 14   The Black Man's Rebuttal   106
(written by Marlon Green)

CHAPTER 15   Who Says Black Men Are Not Faithful?   114
(written by Marlon Green)

CHAPTER 16   Spousal Support   127

CHAPTER 17   The Community Speaks   130

"black men vs. White Men...the Black Woman's Choice"
Foreword
By Joan Adrienne Sturgis,
Editor

Decades ago, when relationships developed between men and women, most often their associations were based upon mutual admiration, respect, similar interests and racial connection. As time passed and the elements of love, devotion, honor, trust and support became an integral part of those relationships, men and women proudly and sacredly vowed to lifetime commitments, and began building strong, loving family units that evolved from one generation to the next.

Yet today, as persistent societal changes threaten, challenge and test family values, more men and women are finding that the cohesive foundations that held their family trees together, years ago, are now lying in shambles like fallen houses of cards.

Sadly enough, for many men and women, family values have become insignificant, meaningless and to some, even a joke. As cheating, indiscriminate sex and one-night stands become the 'games' on any given day, and men and women fall in and out of love like adolescents going through stages of puppy love, it's no wonder relationships are receiving such a blistering black eye. And then, of course, by the time you throw in such elements as couples' low and degrading public displays, demeaning and dirt-slinging criticisms, or the all too common neglect and disregard of innocent children derived from tarnished and broken relationships, you have an up close and personal look at just a small sector of the underlying causes for the negative ways many men and women view and treat one another. And, to their detriment, it is not a pretty picture.

To understand many of the various reasons why so many 'black" men and women tend to be at tremendous odds with one another in their relationships, one merely needs to read ***"black men vs. White Men... the Black Woman's Choice," by authors Cicely J and Marlon Green***. It is a viewpoint from both sides of the coin that needs to be examined.

"black men vs. White Men... the Black Woman's Choice," a no-holds barred reading, is certain to create a firestorm of controversy for its critical and razor-sharp assessment of the unraveling of Black America. This book is a "must-read" that will, undoubtedly, anger those who just might happen to see their own reflections in the authors' mirror that also exposes the issues that continue to broaden the gap between black men and women.

PREFACE

"black men vs. White Men: the Black Women's Choice" is about real life circumstances that are plaguing African American communities throughout this country. I am far from being alone when I say there are close to no single, eligible black men available for our successful Nubian sisters, today. More and more black women are falling for their "Mr. Right," who happens to be characteristically blonde-haired and blue-eyed, because Darnell, DaQuan, Omar, and Tyrone are not equipped to meet her halfway in a relationship. And if, by chance, she meets an eligible black man who is educated and on her level, chances are he's interested in white women, doesn't want to commit, or is "on the DL" (down-low). These are the situations that black women are facing on a day-to-day basis.

More women are opting to have children out of wedlock and rear their offspring alone because there are fewer available men who are willing to make families anymore. The numbers are astronomical. The fact also remains that, these days, more and more black men are getting arrested than getting degrees. This further slims down the pickings for black women.

We have men with multiple "baby mamas" who just don't own up to their responsibilities and women want to feel special, not like they belong to a harem. The African American race is slowly dwindling away as women are forced to date, marry, and procreate with non-black men. Soon, there will be no more African Americans but an entire new race of mixed breeds because other than jail, a basketball court, or a hotel room, black men are nowhere to be found.

Please relax as you take a look at the chapters of my new non-fiction, "black men vs. White Men, the Black Woman's Choice." We are going to take a casual stroll through the major reasons why I feel there are so few eligible black men in our community. I read a lot and I write even more. At times I have come across books written by individuals who try to come off so overly educated with words and intimidating sentences that it becomes hard to enjoy the book because every stance needs to be interpreted. While I may have had the opportunity to go to college and study English literature, I'm fully aware that not everyone else has had that same opportunity. And that could even apply to those who don't want to pick up a book to read at their leisure, because the author has made the reading process as difficult to break down as Shakespeare. I believe in breaking things down to their lowest common denominator; by using plain old English so that anyone reading this can understand. This is not a textbook, nor is it "The Law According to Cicely." A lot of it is my opinion and some is the opinion of others but, to me, since I wrote it, it's true; no matter how ugly it may seem.

Does Life Imitate TV or Does TV Imitate Life?

During my research and examination process for this book, I started noticing a trend. A lot of times television imitates real life but I began to notice, during this particular time period, that real life was imitating television; hence, the run of the hit sitcom, *A Different World.*

A Different World was a spinoff of the popular 80's family, the Cosby's. *The Cosby Show* was a very positive sitcom that displayed to the world how affluent, college educated, upper middle class black families lived. I remember hearing debates, all of the time, about *The Cosby Show* because most white people assumed families like the Cosby's simply did not exist. In my corner of the Universe, families like the Cosby's were everywhere. My dad was the neighborhood Cliff Huxtable with his fancy, colorful sweaters and dry humor. My mom was the epitome of Claire walking into the house with her briefcase in hand after being in meetings with the State of California executives all day, and going right into the kitchen to bake a chicken and to cook some green beans; if my dad hadn't already started dinner. My first introduction to the "black family" was my family, and it wasn't unlike the images I saw every Thursday night on the Cosby Show.

As I left middle school and entered high school, I became attached to the new show *A Different World.* This show was about Denise Huxtable going away to college and her new life and friends at Hillman College. I never missed an episode and couldn't wait 'til I graduated from high school so I could go to a school just like Hillman. College admissions among African American students were at an all time high during this time period, so I guess I wasn't the only black student frequenting this show.

Then, the unthinkable happened. All of the freshmen became seniors, and it was only a matter of time before the show that made me want to do better in school was approaching its final bow. It was 1993, the year I graduated from St. Pat's, when I heard Whitley Gilbert-Wayne announce to her husband, Dwayne Wayne, that she was pregnant. They were leaving for Japan for Dwayne's new job and only reruns would follow that announcement.

Now, here we are, a decade and a half later and there is more of a decline in college admissions than an incline. I decided to crunch some numbers because I wanted to learn a little more about our people, our education, and our future. I chose to research the time period of my age group; those born in the mid-to-late 70s, who were entering college in or around the early to mid 90s, getting advance degrees in the early 2000s, and starting their careers. While the stats may be a little different for enrollees today, I want to focus on the would-be eligible suitors for the professional women I talked to when this book was just an idea and no words had yet been written. Most, if not almost all of my single girlfriends have attended and/or graduated from college.

In most cultures it is a well known fact that many people date and marry their intellectual equal; meaning, most college graduates marry other college graduates. Most professional men in corporate America marry other professionals. You tend to mate with those you see and who are around you, or the people in your immediate circle. If I notice a trend of the college enrollees in the late 90's and early 2000's, it does not surprise me why 70% of black women in my age group are single. In my age group, during this time period, many of our black men were not accompanying us on the college campuses.

In the following pages, I want to talk about the decline in relational values between black men and women. Some of you may be offended, some appalled, some surprised, and some glad that someone is actually willing and brave enough to talk about it. This book is not written to offend anyone. It is written to open up a dialogue between black men and women, with the hopes of healing our relationships. In order for cancer to be expelled from the body, it must first be exposed.

Why Black Women Can't Seem to Find Eligible black men

Notice the words "black men" in the title are in lower-case, while everything else is in caps. Respect for the black man is no longer there. In today's society, everyone is always looking for somebody. Women want a man who can take care of them emotionally, financially, sexually, mentally, and spiritually. Men want a woman who can satisfy their sexual desires, cook a good meal, and get along with their mother. Ultimately, men and women want the same things in the end, but timing and communication often block African American relationships from reaching those goals.

While there are plenty of black men to choose from, the quality lacks in the pickings. Why is it so hard for us to find these eligible men? Here are a few reasons:
- A large percentage of our black men are incarcerated
- Black men lack the tools and knowledge to form complete honest commitments
- So many black men are raised in single parent households headed by their mothers or grandmothers, so they have no clue how to be a man to their woman

- Black men have not mastered the art of how to be faithful
- Black men want a woman who can take care of/carry him
- Black men have given up on the black woman because they consider her to be disrespectful
- Black men ultimately don't know what they want
- Black men mature 10 years behind everyone else
- Most educated black men with a little bit of money want white or Latina women
- This new fad of being "on the DL," and men sleeping with men and not considering themselves gay or bi-sexual has become an epidemic and, frankly, black women are afraid.

There are a number of other reasons why it is so hard for black women to find eligible black men. The above-mentioned ones barely scratch the surface. Most educated, attractive, independent black women don't want to be bothered with the drama associated with "catching" an eligible black man. You have to deal with the other women who want him and he knows this, so he takes forever to commit. If it is marriage you ultimately seek, you have to keep it to yourself because any mention of the "M" word is a sure way to scare off a black man.

You have to be careful at how much you attain as a single black woman because if you make too much you do one of two things: scare off an eligible black man who is insecure about your achievements and net worth, or you attract some loser who sees you as his meal ticket. At any rate, once you reach a certain status it is hard to find your equal; especially, the fact being that more African American females finish college than our male counterparts.

And finding one that has good credit, owns a home, or has a 401K is even a greater challenge. Women are looking for longevity, the future, our potential children, etc., right off the bat. How many times has a black woman gone out with a black man and had a great date, and she then goes home and writes her name with his last name to see how it sounds together. We all do it. It's so natural.

We are taught from the time we are little girls to remain a lady, let him court you and, when the right one comes along, marry him! He, on the other hand, is taught the opposite: date as many as you can, don't spend your money on them because they're all gold diggers, strap it up because she will try to get pregnant on purpose if you have a lil sumthin' sumthin,' and play the field with all the hoes until you get tired. Then, when you are all used up, go to church and find yourself a nice, lil' virgin.

The rules are not the same for men and women; never have been and never will be. There is a serious disconnect in communication because we are looking to settle down and have families, and our men aren't interested in the same thing.

So, women have had to go out and get educated. We have had to educate ourselves in order to survive and stay in this game we call life. We proved we are smart, tenacious, and can persevere, so now we are managers, supervisors, presidents, and CEOs of large corporations. We own our own homes, drive our own Jags and Mercedes-Benzes, we take our own exotic trips to Cancun and the Caribbean, we dine out at the finest restaurants with our girlfriends, and we even buy our own diamonds and furs. And now that the manufacturers have finally gotten it right, we also have been able to pleasure ourselves with the most natural feeling vibrators and dildos. (Did I fail to mention that this is not a spiritual book written to the Saints?) I have to make these disclaimers, sometimes, because I am a pastor's daughter. But I will still keep it 100% real!) Okay, you can read on now.

The black man is hardly needed now by the black woman. And when we feel that we need to be comforted, held, taken out and courted, then we have resolved to (a) experiment with other women or (b) go out with white men; both of which have become more appealing than dealing with yet another dead beat, looking-for-a-meal-ticket, afraid-to-commit, black man.

Black Women and White Men: What Is Really Going On?

Black man, I blame me. I listened to my mother when she told me to go to school, get good grades, be smart, and go to college. She told me to get a degree in higher education and 'never depend on some man to take care of you.' So, I listened, I went to school, I got the degree, and landed that job.

I paid attention to the trends with women's liberation and the movement that taught us to be independent and not submissive. They moved us out of the home and into the factories, sold us cigarettes and told us we didn't have to wear dresses and aprons every day.

We got educated, with BA's, Masters, PhDs and other degrees. We put off dating and marriage because we wanted to be independent. All types of government programs were set aside so we could go to school and get an education. They told us that we had it made, "you're a double minority so you can go to school almost free!" I almost became a professional grant writer because of how convenient it was to be a smart black girl. But while we were so busy going to school to learn about America and finance, the black men in our neighborhoods were being left behind. You, black man, were introduced to drugs, pimps, and a get-rich-quick lifestyle while we were conjugating verbs and dissecting frogs. You were dating all of the other girls in the neighbborhood so that if I wanted to be with you I had to deal with your three baby mamas.

Now we have a huge disparity between our college educated females and our would-be suitable mate: the African American man. We out-number you, some say, 3:1, while more recent studies show its closer to 5:1. But it seems like every time I hear a black man's odds, its 2:1. Can someone please tell us the truth? If it's really 2:1, as you say, then why are so many of us single? 70% single vs. a ratio of 2:1 just doesn't add up, no matter how many times I try to process it in my mind.

Tell me, black man, what do you want us to do? We see you choose white women over us, every day. We grin and bear it, and keep on pushing, even when we know we want to settle down and be married, too. As a result, we are dating, marrying, and procreating with white men. And take note, we're not doing it as often as you are with white women, but our numbers are escalating every year.

So we need to talk! This is a conversation, black man. The dialogue is open and we want to know exactly how you feel. Do you love us enough to try and work out our differences, and forge strong family units; or should we just continue on our quest for happiness and, thus, sleep with your enemy?

CHAPTER 1

Black Men in Jail vs. Black Men in College

A study, done by Global Black News (GBN), showed that there were 603,000 black men in college in 2001, while 791,000 black men were in jail during that same time. So, the reality is, there was more money spent on incarcerations than on higher education.

Black men have experienced a startling reversal of fortunes in the span of only one generation. In 1980, African American men enrolled in higher education out-numbered those incarcerated by a quarter-million. In 2000, black men behind bars exceeded those on campus by 188,000.

U.S. Department of Justice statistics from 2001 indicate that 179,500 black men, ages 18-24, are in prison and jail. Therefore, in the 18-24 age groups, the college/imprisoned ratio for black males are 2.6 to 1.

Prison Population Exceeds Two Million

According to another Department of Justice report released in July 2003, the U.S. prison population surpassed 2 million. For the first time, according to the latest statistics available, 2,166,260 people were incarcerated in prisons or jails at the end of 2002. Since 1990, the U.S. prison population, already the world's largest, has almost doubled.

About two-thirds of prisoners were in state and federal prisons, while the rest were in local jails. The report does not count all juvenile offenders, but noted that there were more than 10,000 inmates, under age 18, held in adult prisons and jails in 2002. The number of women in federal and state prisons reached 97,491.

About 10.4% of the entire African-American male population in the United States, aged 25 to 29, was incarcerated; by far the largest racial or ethnic group. By comparison, 2.4% of Hispanic men and 1.2% of white men, in that same age group, were incarcerated. According to a report by the Justice Policy Institute in 2002, the number of black men in prison has grown to five times the rate it was twenty years ago. Today, more African-American men are in jail than in college. To reiterate, in 2001 there were 791,600 black men in prison and 603,032 enrolled in college. In 1980, there were 143,000 black men in prison and 463,700 enrolled in college.

For their white male counterparts, the ratio is 28 to one. In 2000, there were 3,522,392 white men ages 18-24 enrolled in college, which represents 32.8% of that age group, while 125,700 were in prison in 2001.

Now, while the numbers for black men in college seem to be large, only 35% of these college enrollees actually walk the line and graduate. Does this make for an eligible mate; a college dropout who will find himself in a low paying job, blaming "the man" because he didn't get his sheepskin, and then looking for a smart, degreed, independent black woman who is stupid enough to take care of him? Now, these men are smart. I mean, they were smart enough to get themselves enrolled in college, but too lazy to work hard enough to graduate. It is also possible that their families didn't have the necessary resources, or they were there on athletic scholarships, hurt themselves, couldn't play the sport anymore, and lost his funding. Whatever the unfortunate reasons, these men did not graduate and we are supposed to look at them and consider marrying them simply because they are black and from our community. I don't think so.

These college-aged men ranging from 18 to 24, who have dropped out of college, are added to the list of men of the same age range who will end up behind bars, dead, or strung out on drugs. So, as black women, what are we supposed to do? We are supposed to tell our brothers, our cousins and our sons, since we are raising them alone anyway, that the only way the cycle can be broken and the generational curse can end is by being educated. And that means, not street smarts but book smarts. Some type of post high school education is needed.

I am an advocate for education because, once it's obtained, no one can take away that knowledge. Am I a nerd, a goody-goody, or a smart ass because my parents reared me with the expectation of college? Should I expect, desire, or accept less in a mate because there are more of us than them? Why can't a black woman have her cake and eat it too? Why do we have to choose between family and career, when most of us want both?

And believe it or not, black man, the white man is not your enemy; it is yourselves. Eight out of ten of the murders committed by black men are towards other black men. That leaves 10% for police-related killings and 10% for others. The only hate crimes you hear of today are about us hating each other.

I read an article by Jonathan Tilove, where he examined the absence of black men. Most of these black men are missing because they are dead or in jail. Nationwide, black women out-number black men by 2 million. Where is the future of black America if the ones who are left, don't want us, don't want better for themselves, or think that marriage is for punks and sissies? The reasons black men are not eligible mates for our Nubian sisters are piling up. Are you still questioning why black women are marrying white men and, in some instances, choosing to love each other?

CHAPTER 2

Black Men and Commitments

Black men have mastered the art of non-committal relationships with black women. Unfortunately, we have allowed them to do that and, truth be told, I cannot totally blame the men although they have taken full advantage of the situation. Now we all know that black women out-number black men 5 to 1. I am going to keep repeating those odds over and over again until it sounds redundant so people will stop calling me a traitor and a disgrace to the race for telling black women to date "others." She does not need my permission, anyway. All she needs to know is that we understand if she makes the conscientious decision to throw in the towel and says "to hell with it."

I will not speak for every black woman in America. Some of them have wonderful husbands, boyfriends, and baby daddies. On the other hand, there are still a large percentage of black women who are single, alone, lonely, confused, upset, bewildered, and wondering: *Why did I spend so much time going to school and working hard to have a better life if I have to live it alone?* At what price, other than tuition, does a black woman pay when she has achieved too much? She has paid for it with her life, her future, the husband she doesn't have and the children she might never know. Some of us think that's a price too damn high to pay.

Some women would actually prefer to have a piece of a man rather than no man at all. There used to be a time when women would hold out from having sex until there were talks of marriage or, at least, a solid commitment. These days, men can easily get sex on the first date because so many women are lonely and vulnerable; it can go on like this for weeks, months, and even years before he makes a decision of commitment; if he makes one at all. So many couples are opting to live together rather than getting married for whatever their reasoning may be. To the black man, I ask, when did this become okay? You have to get a license for a dog but when it comes to your woman, you choose to just live with her. You expect her to act like your wife and perform wife-like duties but when it comes to making her your actual bride, that's just totally out of the question.

For couples who agree to this nonconventional way of co-habitation, I have nothing to say. I mean, that is strictly your business if you would rather just live with a man than to be someone's wife. I will say that this new attitude of "shacking up," being a way of life or consideration for a family, has made it tremendously hard for the women who look forward to having an actual, traditional family. Just as men aren't in a hurry to marry, women are just as afraid to be vocal about their expectations of marriage.

The fact that women out-number men by such a large gap is a scary realization for most women. If we are not on our "best behavior" 90% of the time, we are in fear of being replaced by some woman who does not expect as much. Expecting marriage is expecting too much so we can either agree to date these men for ten years and have two of his illegitimate children, or we can leave him alone and find ourselves single, with no children, at 40.

Some of these women are opting for the former and now we have an over abundance of households where mom and dad are together, but not married. This is not a good example we are setting for the generation that is to follow after us.

Some men will play the emotional game with women by claiming, "If it ain't broke, don't fix it." Like the fact that their mere presence should be enough. This behavior is beyond ludicrous and it is downright disrespectful. Any woman, who would allow men to have this kind of attitude with them, makes it hard for the women who want real families and not a make believe one.

If you live with a man, he has absolutely no reason in the world to marry you. So if it is marriage you ultimately want, then you should move out and find a real man who wants a real woman and a real relationship 'cause, sister-girl, he ain't the one."

Excuse me, but I had to go there for a minute because this bothers me. If both parties are cool with living together and not being married then, as I said earlier, that's their business. However, in most shacking situations, more often than not, the woman wants to be married and not have a "roommate." Sadly, she may go along with it because she knows she won't be getting a proposal.

Then we have the brothers who think it is fashionable to father children outside of wedlock. Okay, after the first "slip up," we realize it could have been a mistake or an accident. But some of these non-commitment making bastards are fathering 3, 4, and 5 children with multiple women and they don't see anything wrong in that. And for you trifling men who have 2, 3, and 4 children, all with the same woman and you still haven't married her, I'm not sure who's dumber, you or her.

Not mentioning names, but rappers, producers, ball players, actors and many other black men in the public eye who have children by multiple women, while proclaiming to be single, come to mind. Our young men are looking up to this and thinking it's a normal way of life. It is now a badge of honor to have more than one baby mama.

To me, it's embarrassing. This is all America thinks of us. We are nothing more than horny, immature, niggas, making all these babies, and then going on public assistance because no one is equipped to financially care for them. And, for those men who do work hard and provide for their children and "<u>ALL</u>" of the mothers, big ups to you!

It still doesn't change the fact that fathering all these children with all these different women is emotionally and physically unhealthy for the children, their mothers, and yourselves.

Black men need to be made accountable for their actions, and we have given them a free pass. Society doesn't expect much from them because they haven't shown us much. The ignorant ones will defend their behavior, the militant ones will blame someone else usually "whitey" or "the man," and the typical ones will point the finger at the black woman.

I am here to give the black woman's point of view. I do not speak for each and every one, but I speak for some. However, to be fair, my co-author, Marlon Green, will offer his perspective on behalf of the black male because there are two sides to this story and they both deserve to be heard.

The black man is so afraid of appearing weak to his feminine counterpart that he holds all of his emotions inside and hopes she will stick around to tolerate his immature ways. Men, by nature, gravitate toward things they know they can succeed at and move away from things that are possible for them to fail at. Thus, marriage has become an institution of the past.

Our enslaved ancestors, who were not allowed to legally marry, would be so disappointed to know that we are now able to love freely and enjoy one another, and marriage is the furthest thing from our mind.

I have a funny feeling toward any man in his late 30s to early 40s who is not married, has not thought about marriage, has never been married, or thinks he is better off alone. God did not intend for it to be that way. He said 'it is not good for man to be alone' so he made woman. He also went on to say that 'a man, who finds a wife, finds a good thing and gains favor with the Lord.' My first inclination is that he may be gay. And, if I pay particularly close attention, I soon come to realize that he might possibly just be a whore.

Black men have turned away from their religious roots and upbringing, and have embraced their own philosophies on life and how they choose to live it. As a result, it has diminished the morale of our communities, our families, and the generations that are to follow us.

Our young black boys haven't a clue about what the word commitment really means, because they don't see black marriages in their neighborhood. Even back in the day, the older television shows like *Good Times* showed a struggling black family, but the father was there. It was hard on the Evans family, but James was there to support Florida and their 3 children. I loved *The Jeffersons*! To this day, I still watch the reruns, sometimes. George could have left home and got him a white woman when he made it, but he stayed with Weezy because he loved her and she was there for him from the beginning. There are no family programs like that on television today. Everyone is divorced or the families are blended.

We had *All of Us*; they were divorced and had to come up with a way to balance Bobby's life with both his mother and father. We had *Girlfriends,* where Maya couldn't stay with her husband for an entire season and, when Toni finally got married, she married a white doctor and not one of the many black men she had been dating since the show debuted.

Now this is television and fictional, but everything we see on TV bears some truth to how life really was during that time. Today, we have a bunch of fake "reality" shows, where we have people searching for love and commitment, and demeaning themselves and each other simply for ratings. As I cringe, trying to watch, I have come to the realization that most of these people have no idea what true love is. They don't love themselves but are making spectacles of themselves on national television by crying and begging someone they barely know to choose them.

What is this teaching our young people? It's sad, it's scary, and it explains a lot of what is going on in relationships that are not weekly publicized on BET, VH1, and I certainly don't want to leave out Bravo. If reality shows are to display what is real, then I am further saddened and disgusted at what they choose to show the world as it pertains to black men and women, and how we relate to each other. We have so much more to offer but have resorted to this type of classless display for white America to sit back and laugh at. We have come so far, but it appears to me that we are being pushed back nearly as far back as we have come.

The positive change has to start within the family. Let us not forget, however, that black families are becoming more complicated than Chinese checkers. Some black men lack the tools to fully commit. To them, life as it pertains to dating is a smorgasbord, and there are too many women to have to choose just one. They seem to lack the knowledge it takes to sustain the needs of a mature black woman. All a black woman wants is a man to "love her *right*." It's not about the almighty dollar, how big his anatomy is, or what kind of car he drives. We are so past the materialistic aspects when it comes to loving a man.

Can you catch me if I fall? Will you have my back when the world seems to be against me? Do you pay your bills on time? Can I, at least, communicate with you on an adult level about something other than sex? The frustration is overwhelming, at times. What do we do to stop this and encourage these black men to either commit or leave us the hell alone?

CHAPTER 3

How Does a Black Woman Raise a Black Man Alone?

While a black woman raising a young black male alone was never intended to be the ideal makeup of the family unit, this is a situation that has become all too common. So many women have been left to rear their children without a father in the home that it is almost an expectation that most black men come from families where there are absentee fathers.

How does this happen? Men are getting women pregnant and not facing up to their responsibilities. They are leaving the roles of both mother and father solely on the black woman, and that is hardly fair. Not only is it an injustice to the single mother, but it is just as unfair to those children who are left without a father and/or male role model.

Now some men are stepping up to the plate and acting as fathers to their children. They show up to school outings, they pay child support, and they are active figures in their children's lives, but they have made the decision to not marry the mother of the child(ren), which still makes the child a bastard/illegitimate.

Who made this right? Who said it was okay to father a child and not marry the mother? If men would be men, raise their sons, and be positive role models in the lives of their children, then black women would have better options when it comes to finding an eligible mate once these young males grow up. Society, or the black community, has condoned having children out of wedlock and, thus, we have a generation of bastards who will be in control of our country's future one day.

This epidemic is sickening, and those who partake in it are less than deserving of any type of respect. Then, we have the ones who actually go through with marriage but their marriages never seem to last. It is easier to find a gun in school, a college graduate on welfare, or a gay man in church than it is to find a long lasting, happy, black married couple who are not in their 70's. What's sad about this is the fact that it's so expected.

By society's expectations of us, we are not expected to marry. They don't want us to raise our children together because that shows strength. We have been programmed to be against each other and to be non-supportive of one another when things are not all good. And, once again, the dumb-ass black man continues to fall for it.

He will come up with reason after reason why he won't commit to marry and provide for the mother of his children. Can we blame him, though? His father wasn't around either, so the cycle just simply continues. For the black man who was raised by a single mom, the true sense of family is foreign to him. So, unfortunately, his son will grow up to learn that his father was less than a man. Not necessarily because he was not around for him, but because his father allowed another man to love his mother the way he should have been there to love her. He allowed the next man, sometimes non-black, to marry his children's mother because he lacked the knowledge needed to fight the curse and create a successful black family in the community.

When will we begin to learn that this was how it was set up to be? Are black men really that stupid to sit back and allow negative predictions to come true without even trying to fight their relevance? As fake as I believe the Willie Lynch letter was, it is troubling that we are self-fulfilling the prophecy this fictitious character created. It was written, I believe, as an eye opener for us. Instead of reading it and taking heed, we have used it as our roadmap for life.

We are separate and divided, and the only times we can seem to get along are when we are in the clubs or at church. For some reason we just can't seem to make it work in the home. I am trying to find out why this is, but I need some help.

There are more black babies born into single parent homes today than in two-parent, married households. When I began the research for this book, the statistic stood at 68%. As I began to edit and rewrite, I ran across a more current statistic on *Storm Front* which suggested it is now closer to 80%. Whatever the correct number might be, it is still astronomically high and a figure that cannot be ignored.

I guess this is why so many of our black men end up in prisons and penitentiaries instead of in politics and pulpits, because they resort to crime to help mama with the bills, buy the newest Jordan's, or to sport the latest designer fashions they see rappers wearing in their most current videos.

Black men should be ashamed of themselves. Any black man who is walking around with children and is not married to the mother and/or is not financially responsible for his offspring should feel like less than a man because he is doing exactly what white America has always said he would do.

Back during the time of slavery, even as slave masters were sleeping with their black female slave, they would allow a black man to impregnate his black woman, but he wouldn't permit him to marry her. He also would not allow the black man to be there for her or her children, and would force the female slave to go on public assistance. He knew this and planned it that way because, every opportunity he got, he slept with her, impregnated her, and then, shunned and refused to care for his mulatto children.

He may have let the lighter-skinned child work in the house rather than in the field, but he felt no sense of kinship or responsibility to her.   Because of this mental and emotional raping of our ancestors, black women have become accustomed to having children with a man and not planning or expecting a commitment or sense of family from him. All she wants is child support. "Just let this child work in your kitchen, Massa."

This process was all part of the divide and conquer plan on the plantation. They figured if they programmed it on our mind to not expect anything from our men, such as not allowing us to marry and have babies with him, for generations to come, the black family would continue to be divided. And, guess what, they were right. They said it before it happened and it's still occurring today. Is it psychological and non-fixable or will we be able to read the pre-written script and decide to rewrite it?

Of course, white America doesn't want to see black love, black marriage, and black babies. These elements of the black family are a show of black strength and the white man does not want that. And, now that it is allowed black men are preventing this power. Does that make any sense?

So now the very race who kept us from being a family unit is trying to create family units with us. White men love black women now, more than ever, and black men are sitting back and allowing their queens to be loved by people who used to be considered their enemy. And the black woman loves it because that white man has good credit, drives a nice car, and he knows his role in the family. If she wants to stay home and take care of the children she can because he's educated and employed enough to provide for the family. So, do we trade all that in to come back home to you; the man who will not commit, will not work, and will not marry us?

Instead of black men recognizing the problem and delving within themselves for solutions, they look at black women with their white men, with contempt, like she has the plague or is dating him out of spite. Truth be told, black women who date white men do not have an exclusivity rule against black men. The white man is available to her. He treats her the way she wants to be treated. She feels appreciated when she is out with him.

In most cases she would feel the same if she were given the opportunity to be with a black man who wants the same things she does. On the other hand, it seems to me it is just the contrary for black men who date white women. A lot of black men who date white women have had a pattern or history of exclusively dating white women. Look at their last three girlfriends before their current one. The black guy who dates and marries white women is typically the same type of guy who, at the end of the day, most assertive black women don't want him anyway.

One woman said she felt as though men who date and marry white women are subconsciously gay. I can't say that I agree with this statement 100%, but this is simply one of the perceptions black women have, when it comes to the dating   issues we are having with our men. This is not a way for black women to get back at black men.

We sat back and waited to get noticed but not only did you start dating white girls, as soon as your family and friends became comfortable with the idea, you started marrying her. While we can't be bitter, or upset that we were left out of the selection pool for being too nappy, too thick, or too opinionated, we can be upset that you have now categorized us in a most negative way. You have shared this information with your now white wife/girlfriend, and she uses it against us every day in the workforce; so now we are constantly on the defense. In the   meantime, white women are looking at us, gloating, while still trying to be and look like us through the use of weaves, collagen, and butt implants.

They know black men don't want us anymore, and they are standing there grinning and holding up their prizes for all to see. Black men put us on the defense with white women on the daily and if she says something out of line and we slap her in the mouth, we're the ones who get fired; not Buffy.

Black men thought we were too nappy, so we got relaxers and, when our hair wasn't flowing past our shoulders, we got weaves. To look even more European, we started wearing colored contacts and we even changed our eating habits to be more healthy and slim because you seemed to no longer delight in our curves that everyone else seems to covet. That is, until Beyonce' popped up and reassured us that it was still sexy to be bootylicious.

Pitiful, pitiful, black men! Our self esteem is slowly diminishing and it almost gives the black woman cause not to even want to look in your direction. Why should we? All you seem to want is one thing from us and a commitment is not it. We yield to the pressure and temptation and then what? So we have your kid and thrive on the promise that you are going to be there and we will be a family. That is not your intention, however, and truth be told once again, it never really was.

Black men make empty promises to us in order to stay out of court. Then, after all is said and done and he has moved on, we are still the ones left to pick up the pieces and to raise his child. And, God forbid you show up to pick up the child and you have the other woman in the car. Just put salt on the open wound, why don't you? I call that emotional abuse, while some simply call it playing games.

Ask any single mother, it is hard rearing children alone. It is embarrassing enrolling your five-year old in kindergarten and his last name is different from yours. It is difficult trying to figure out which child belongs to which mother, because their last names don't match, anymore. The father isn't around. He doesn't want to be married, but it is naturally assumed that the child is to take on his family name. I don't think that's right. If a child's parents are not married, I believe the child should have the last name of the mother since, in most cases, she is the primary caregiver, anyway. Let the dead-beat dad be the one to be embarrassed when his child asks why his last name is different.

Mothers are tired of having to explain that she had a baby with a man who was determined to make her a statistic and not a wife. That is why so many women are opting to give their last name to their child, because the men they have formerly dealt with, don't deserve to have their name carried on. They are not men, so they are not needed.

If I have to choose between having a baby by a black man, who won't marry me, and marrying a white man and having some little mixed curly-headed children, then I will go with the latter. The lifestyle of these certain black men is a disgusting habit and if we women are equipped, only we can change the way things are going. I say, leave their asses alone and find another man who will treat you like the black queen, princess, and woman you are.

If he happens to be of a different ethnic background, given her dating history, I think we all would understand. And if this "other" man wants to love you and the black man can't or just won't, tell him to go kick rocks and he can read about you and your new man in Jet magazine's "Love and Happiness" section. And, yes, they do feature interracial couples!

Classic Baby Mama Syndrome

So ladies, he didn't marry you when you had the first baby, so why in the hell are you pregnant again? Some women think that a baby will change him, for the better, and make him want to be with you. Let's not be naïve, here. These men don't care if you have 3, 4, or 5 children by him; marriage is the furthest thing from his mind because there will always be another chicken-head or pigeon-brained girl who thinks it's cute to be with a man with children, who bad mouths their mother and makes no commitment to her.

She feels as though she has won some type of prize when, in essence, she's suffering from a case of low self-esteem. Therefore, I'm not going to waste any ink, space, or time addressing these females because they are not worthy of my time. They need to work on themselves and try to find a man who is not attached and has no children.

Maybe then these fathering boys will go home and marry the mothers of their offspring since no other woman, with any self respect, will be bothered with such a dead-beat of a man. Don't get me wrong or take me for a hypocrite, when I say that I do agree some women just aren't wife material. She may be pretty, can give some really good lovin' and can make an incredibly tasty ham sandwich, but she lacks the tools to create a productive family life.

Okay then, I can understand why you are reluctant to marriage but 9 times out of 10, this is not the case as to why black men are not marrying their "sex partners." To reiterate, once more, most black men just do not want the responsibility of a commitment. We are letting them get away with it by sleeping with them and not making them accountable to us, first. We are all guilty of it and I, for one, cannot point the finger at anyone because I am no angel. So, I will give a pass, just this once, to the stand-up men who take care of their children, no matter how many mothers gave birth to them. If you are financially responsible for your offspring, then I applaud your efforts. However, it does not excuse the fact that it is unhealthy to produce multiple babies with "hella" women.

I am a woman, I was born a girl and I only know how to be a female. How then can I successfully teach a male child how to be a man? I can't. I can only tell him what I think, show him what I expect, and tell him how women want to be treated, but I honestly cannot show him how to be a man. I can feed him well so he grows and matures at a normal pace, and I can help him become successful, but I cannot teach him how to point and shake, because I squat and wipe.

There are some things that only a man can teach another man so, because these fathers aren't around, mothers are improvising and we have a generation of angry, violent, mixed up, and sexually confused males. You can place the blame wherever you want. This is my book, I wrote it, and these are my thoughts and feelings, so I choose to blame black men; all black men; every last one of you.

If you are non-committal, you are at fault. If you are an unwed father, you are at fault. If you *live* with your girlfriend but your dog has a license, you are at fault. If you are over 35, have been in a serious relationship with a woman for over a year, and have not even thought of marrying her, you are at fault. Plain and simple, you are just at fault for being black.

Needless to say, I am fed up to the max with black men; all of you. I hear your ignorant comments on the Bart train; I see you on the corner with your pants saggin' down to your knees; I smell you in the liquor store smelling like herbs and spices and then, I go to church and see the gay one in the choir winking at the one making a joyful noise unto the Lord on the organ. I even see the preacher in the pulpit salivating over the single women as his first lady of the church is sitting on the front pew, and I see the newly saved one, just released from prison, who now is looking for a good church girl. No one is above my wrath.

And for those of you who are married to black women, have black children (all by the same woman), work full time, and take care of your households, then kudos to you. Unfortunately, you are rare. This book is not about you and there were no stats on the internet I could refer to in order to mention you. Your trifling friends, however, are all over the place; they are basketball and football players; rappers and entertainers; well-to-do businessmen, and college educated politicians.

Any black man, who is not loyal to his black woman, can deem himself guilty based on my findings. It is my intention to make people aware. I want to raise an eyebrow. I want to strike a nerve and make you upset, because the only emotion a black man gives freely, without much coaxing, is anger. I am sure this book will take him there. I hope it makes him think after he has read it. But, then again, I almost forgot, black men don't read so I'm going to have to depend on my sisters to share this with their boyfriends, baby daddies, fiancés, and, for those of you who have them, husbands.

CHAPTER 4

Black Men Are Not Faithful!!

Why is it that you cannot find a black man, successful or otherwise, who is faithful to one woman? Even the best of the best, the crème de la crème, at one point or another, has cheated on his wife or girlfriend. We all understand that women outnumber men. The ratio was mentioned before. But does that excuse men to philander around with as many women as they choose? When you are committed to someone, you are faithful to them. Even on bad days when you are mad at one another, you still value your relationship and refuse to mess around with any other female.

The only reason why it worked with our grandparents is because our grandmothers had nowhere else to go. They had no education, no jobs, no skills; they just took care of the house while Papa slept around town. That's why we have cousins all over the country. Ever think about that?

There's a new form of cheating going around now. With access to the Internet, you can have a conversation, for hours on end, with someone in another state or country and never leave your computer or laptop. While you may not be sleeping with your cyber-sex partner, you are emotionally cheating on your wife or girlfriend, which is just as damaging. With access to so many forms of cheating and so many types of women, it is hardly surprising that black men will cheat. They will cheat with your girlfriend or the neighbor down the street. It seems to be part of a black man's character to practice infidelity and it has been tolerated far too long.

For those men out there who will argue that they are faithful to their woman or wife, this is not for you. I am addressing only the guilty parties to whom black women have fallen victim. I am referring to the corporate America males who are married, have children and wonderful families. They just can't help themselves. When they see you out, their wedding rings don't exist anymore.

Some single women are so lonely and desperate that many of them don't even care that the man is married with children. They realize that, since single men don't want to commit anyway, why not have affairs with successful married men. He has the money to pay you to keep your mouth shut, in the form of such perks as gifts, trips, money, etc., and you know the only other woman he is probably seeing is his wife. As ridiculous as this may sound, this is what some black women have resorted to. It has become a lifestyle; to be a kept woman by a married man. Personally, it's not what I aspire to be, but I know too many single women who opt for that in lieu of finding a man ready, willing, and able to make an honest woman out of her.

The first thing I know I'm going to hear is someone saying, 'Cicely is a bitter, lonely, and scorned black woman.' I laugh at people who make those assumptions, because that could not be further from the truth. I read, I listen, and I advise. I have so many female acquaintances, not all black, mind you, who talk to me frequently about the cheating habits of their black men. Trust me, ladies, white girls who think they have a prize with our black men get cheated on more than black women do. Black men, who are married to white women and cheat on them, tend to cheat with black women.

I have had my fair share of a cheating man but I only judge the one I am with and not all men. The title of this chapter may seem to be to the contrary, but I don't think that all men cheat. I do, however, believe the majority of black men do and it is accepted, sometimes even expected. If given the opportunity I wholeheartedly believe that men, particularly black men, will cheat. Women cheat, as well; but, for the most part, women need a reason to do it. All men need is a location.

I have dated across the board. I don't limit myself to just one group. I have noticed profound differences between black men and their white counterparts in how they have treated me when dating. Black men, by nature, are defensive. Their guards are up right from the gate. First, they have to go through the entire scrutinizing process to determine if I'm a gold digging-type female.

Back in the day, that was not even an issue because a man felt as though it was his duty to provide and protect. Now black men want roommates; a partner who carries equal shares.

They don't want to be the provider. They want the woman to share the load. They will date several women if that is what it takes to obtain some of the materialistic things they deem important. This steers us into the subject of role reversal, which is a different subject in a different chapter.

Black men try to pattern their lives according to what they see. Whatever the public deems as popular, that is what they want. 'Monkey see, monkey do' is what we used to say as schoolyard children. Rappers, ball players, and politicians are all doing it, so it must be okay. Their irrational sense of thinking is, *They're all married and cheating, and their wives are staying and accepting it, so my wife will stay and accept it, as well.* The reality is, these women feel as though they've hit the jackpot. They marry these men and never have another financial worry in their lives, and cheating comes along with the territory. Their rationale is *He's making $20 million throwing a ball around, so I'm going to sit back and reap all of the benefits.*

The only time all of this really becomes a problem is when these men get sloppy with their behavior and it suddenly becomes public knowledge. Suddenly their women are embarrassed and feel as though they have to leave in order to save face. On the other hand, if they have stayed married long enough and have been lucky enough to pop out a couple kids all is not lost. They will, more often than not, cash in on a really nice, comfortable alimony and child support check; so it's all good.

Everyone is watching this and thinking it's okay. I feel, if a man is cheating then, yes, he should pay up. He is ruining a family and many lives with his actions so he should very well be responsible for that. For those women who stay and accept it, they hurt the women who stand on the premise that cheating is not acceptable.

I, for one, don't want to be with a man who is unfaithful to me. I don't care how many million$ he has and what kind of house he can buy me. I will not stay! It is not okay, ladies and don't let anyone tell you that it is! Black men prey on women with low self-esteem, so they can have the upper hand. If a woman believes no one else will want her then, guess what, no one else will.

I fell victim to that when I was young and in my early 20s. I let a man tell me that I was skinny, not all that, and I would never find someone like him. You know what, he was right. I actually was a little skinny, I never had an "I think I'm all that" attitude, and I was determined when I left, to never allow someone like him to waste my time, ever again. He was the lowest of the low and I have been fortunate enough to have never found another black man like him who thought he was God's gift to women. He had nothing more to offer me than his sex appeal, and I was young, naive and impressionable. I was college educated, had a good job, and was self sufficient. His license was suspended, so I had to pick him up from the bus stop. My prize in return was that I was able to proclaim to my friends that I had a man. I decided after our relationship had run its course, that I would raise the bar. I would only deal with men on my level intellectually, spiritually, emotionally and financially. I assumed that would solve the problem, but soon learned that the more money they make, the worse they are.

There are many different reasons why men cheat, and there are just as many reasons why women defend their cheating ways, such as:

- **_Weight gain_**. Some men are turned off if their woman gains too much weight. He unrealistically thinks that after 10 years and 3 kids, she should still be a perfect size 6. Weight happens. Stretch marks are a part of some women's lives, but this cannot be used as a pass to cheat. It takes a good man to love the person inside and not the outward appearance. It shouldn't matter if the woman you're with is 120lbs. or 220lbs. If you love her, encourage her. If you are not physically or sexually attracted to her with extra weight, then work with her to help her lose it, so she can feel good about herself again. The fact of the matter is that she probably gained the weight because you were cheating. You didn't cheat because she gained the weight. Think about it. This tends to be more of an issue with black men who are in relationships with black women. I have noticed that most black men who are with white women have a tendency to go for the fat, out of shape, fried over-dyed hair, white girl who lives in the local trailer park. One exception, however, is Ice-T's wife, Coco. She's not overweight, but for all intent and purposes, she looks like a tawdry porn star.

- **_Sexual appetite_**. Some women lose their sexual drive after having children. Rearing toddlers is a hard job. I've been there and I did not feel sexy after changing diapers and making bottles all day. These are things that need to be talked about and, communication, unfortunately, is another shortcoming for black men. If you want it all the time and your wife doesn't, then that's a potential problem that needs to be addressed before it gets out of hand. Men will use that as an excuse to cheat every time. They will freely discuss it with the woman they are cheating with but never bring it up to wifey. If she knew your pecker was pointing in another woman's direction, she might be a little more willing to put on some sexy lingerie instead of sweats, and tune you up, more regularly. But, of course, instead of telling her you need more, you simply go search for a substitute and justify it.

- ***Sexual fantasies***. Some black women are not as open with the types of sexual activities other women will indulge in with their husbands. If a man even brings it up, that's grounds for putting him on the couch. While this may be very unfair to the husband, it still doesn't justify his reason for cheating. Once again, marriage is about communication. With that comes compromise. The only advice I can give wives out there is, if you don't give him the sex he wants, someone else will. These sexual habits need to be addressed and discussed before marriage. Make sure you're compatible on all levels before you pledge to spend the rest of your lives together. If that described your husband, "get your freak on" and "rock his world!" I'm not going to tell you how, because there's a book out about that already, better known as "The Vixen Diaries" (2007) by Karrine Steffans. I will say, however, that sometimes we can contribute to the problem when the man has a wandering penis.

- *He's sleeping with his wife still.* Okay, I know this sounds extra ridiculous, but there are women out there in serious and committed relationships with married men. They have property together, cars, and joint bank accounts. Some of these men even father children with these mistresses. These women have the audacity to claim that he is cheating on her because he still sleeps with his wife. These women are foolish and I hate to waste my time speaking on them, but these were some of the points brought up in my poll, so I want to keep it real. If a man is married and dating you, he is cheating on his wife, boo-boo, not you! In a case like this, I'm not sure who's dumber; the man or the mistress. Rarely, does the husband ever leave the wife for the mistress. So, if the wife walks up to you on the street and punches you dead in your face, SORRY, you deserved it!

So whether you are rich or poor, professional athlete or Corporate America, black men have proven time and time again that faithfulness is not something to which they can commit. Womanizing has become a popular sport and black women are on the defense. If you cheat on me and I stay with you, I'm simply showing you what I feel I'm worth.

Love is a choice, not an emotion. There is action behind it. In other words, if a man truly loves you or, at least, says he does, chances are he will not cheat on you. If he does, then it isn't love. If you are just casually dating this man then, by all means, don't put all of your eggs in one basket because you can bet, he surely won't. If he can't give you the attention and affection you need, then keep it moving. By the time he comes around, who knows, you may be married to someone else, more deserving. Just make sure you always have a backup.

When you are dealing with a black man, you have to keep plenty in rotation. When one messes up, don't get mad; just replace him. Black men are no more than accessories. They are like usable toys that we can dispose of when we are tired of them. Why? Because their black asses don't want to commit, so don't give them the satisfaction of calling themselves your man. If he doesn't want to be married, he's just your friend.

You may have sex with him. The sex may actually be good *sometimes,* but never make him think you aren't capable of finding someone else to take his place. If you two don't share the same last name, then it's fair game. The only commitment I recognize is marriage. Ironically, I believe that's the only commitment God recognizes, too.

Never let him have the top spot. That spot is always and only reserved for the husband; the man with enough balls to set a date and make it right. Please make sure your backup includes men of other races. Make sure they have passports and love to travel. When the black man calls to take you out to a movie, make yourself unavailable. He has been taking you to the movies for the last damn five years. Tell him you appreciate his offer for a $10 movie, cold hot dog and a box of stale popcorn, but you are just on your way out the door, headed to Brazil with your other "friend."

CHAPTER 5

Black Men Want to be Taken Care Of

Today Black women have reached a level of success that cannot be denied. We have worked hard to earn our rightful place in society, and some of us have put off marriage and children to pursue other more professional roles. Now that we have attained that degree, got that six-figure job, and are living comfortably in our gated communities, we have a hard time finding a suitable mate. Why, because we are looked at as a meal ticket or a free ride. It seems like once you reach a certain level of success, the pickings become even slimmer.

It's easier for an uneducated black woman on AFDC and Section 8 to get a husband than it is for a woman with a MBA and 401K plan. I'm not belittling any woman on public assistance. It is there to help, so if you need it, by all means, get it, girl. But, why is it that these women have no hard time at all finding suitable mates? Men are readily there to take them from their current economic status and introduce them to a whole new lifestyle.

Intimidated or Irritated: I, for one, do not believe black men are intimidated by black women who are articulate, attractive, and successful. Part of me believes that these men are irritated because a lot of well-to-do single women have that "I don't need a man attitude." Ladies, a man whether he's black, white, or purple needs to feel needed. So, let's be a little honest here. Some of us are single because of our attitudes; not our altitudes. I will say that a lot of black men, who have had to deal with these "I'm every woman" egos, automatically think that all college educated and/or successful black women are like that. They won't even give us a chance.

They think that just because she has so much, she doesn't want or need a man, even though that's not the aura she's giving off. It's almost a catch-22 situation. We are encouraged to go to college, get an education, and be able to take care of ourselves but now that we've done that, we have worked our way right out of the selection process when it comes to black men who actually want us. And then, to be attractive on top of that, black men want someone who is a little easier to impress.

I want to focus on these Oprah-type females and why they are still single at 30, 40, and 50 years old. Thank you, Ms. Winfrey for being our ultimate example for achieving dreams but, now these black men think that since we are educated, accomplished, and successful, we don't want husbands; which, in fact, more often than not, we do. Some say they don't because there are none around to choose from. We don't want anyone to think something's wrong with us because we are single, so we have coined the phrase, "I'm just gonna be like Oprah."

Women don't want to be the head of the household. Women don't want to be financially responsible for a grown man. Women want a man who can come to her equipped to meet her halfway and beyond. Some of us want to be like Michelle, with the black man, the White House, and the brown children. And where is the wrong in that?

I do believe that we have to be there for each other, but I hear too many stories from too many of my single sisters complaining about how dense their pockets have become because they fell in love with the wrong man. Their credit is in jeopardy, they're stressed out, and he does not contribute. Once we reach a certain level of success, we are no longer surrounded by professional men who resemble us. Instead those professionals have blue eyes, blonde or brunette hair, and we call them Blaine, Chad and Ian. There becomes a serious disconnect between professional black women and professional black men. Their interactions seem more like a competition than a partnership. White men don't compete with us. They find no need to. We can come together and focus on love and happiness, instead of which black person in the relationship is going to reach the top of the corporate ladder first.

Then we have the man who clearly wants to be with you based on what you can provide for him. This is so opposite of the original design of family. The wife is the help mate, not the roommate. I don't agree that a woman should pay all the household bills. I think she should help her husband, but he should be the main provider. If she makes more than he does, then the family should live within *his* means; in other words on what he can provide financially to the family. The woman should not control the family with her money. Yet, it happens because, in a lot of cases, we make more than he does, so he wants us to carry the financial load but, at the same time, expects us to be the docile, submissive wife. It doesn't work; not in black families with an aggressive black woman who will tell you where to go and how to get there when you try to flex your muscles as the "man of the house" when she's paying the mortgage.

Is this a direct result of the women's liberation movement? Let me assist. I want to, but don't treat me like a 50/50 partner only when it comes to finances. In every other situation you want to take the lead role and I'm relegated to the background, only until the mortgage is due. Then we have an equal partnership.

Who made up these rules? I believe in supporting my man. I am there whenever he needs me, whether it's mentally, emotionally, spiritually, sexually, or financially. No one should ever have his back more than me. I do believe in chivalry, however, and while I don't need a man to take care of me, the effort would be nice. I don't care if I have $1million and he only has $100. If he's the man in the marriage/relationship, then so be it. Just don't put me in a position where I am taking care of you. A man's bed can get cold, real quick if the woman is the one holding it down; I'm just saying.

I have had my run-ins with men who wanted me to buy them cell phones, co-sign for vehicles, buy suits and put them on my credit cards, etc. Do I look like I have "boo boo the fool" written across my forehead? These men had good paying jobs, but they looked at me as a means of getting what they wanted because I was accomplished and had a good job. I'm not in the habit of taking care of grown men.

Who got your cell phone before I came along? Whose name is on the paperwork of your current car loan, and who bought all of the other suits you've been wearing? If it was another woman then you should have stayed with her. It's not that I'm selfish; I'm just not that foolish anymore.

Why do black men think they can come along and spit all this game to you, and you should open up your legs, your wallet, and your heart (in that order) to be used and then tossed aside?

I had a white friend, and for all intent and purposes, let's call him Bryce. All he wanted to do was wine and dine me, and make sure I was always having a good time when I was with him. He'd come and pick me up and we'd ride up to Reno or Tahoe for the weekend, and it was awesome. He paid for everything; dinners, concerts, and hotel suites, (double occupancy, of course). Whatever we did, he made it clear that it was on him the entire time.

Bryce was so nice to me and seriously interested into what I was into, that a few times I even offered to pay. I pulled out my wallet on more than one occasion to offer to pay, but he insisted he treated every time we went out. He was treating me in a way to which I wasn't accustomed. I was used to men expecting me to pay half the bill or my portion and if you can believe this, some would even ask if I was treating. They'd ask me out on a date and then had the nerve to ask if I was treating! I found better times at home by myself on the weekends watching old movies.

If a guy asks you out and then expects you to pay, you are clearly dating the wrong man. I really liked Bryce and, to be honest, I still like Bryce. I think, though he was ready for marriage, at the time, I really wasn't, so our timing was off. It didn't matter to me that he was white. He was one of the nicest men I had ever dated; not because he paid for everything, but because he made me feel like he cherished our times together. I was important to him and not an afterthought because some other plans fell through.

Then there was Derek. We used to go out, too. If he paid for dinner, he wanted me to take care of the tip. When we'd drive to far off places, he looked to me for gas money. If he took me to a nice restaurant, he expected me to pay the valet. You see where I'm going with this? We would have had an entire relationship of tit-for-tat, had I stayed with him. I was always reaching into my wallet for this and that when we went out. It was irritating. He was supposed to be courting and impressing me, but I soon got over the 6' 4" Derek and moved on. Oh, how I missed Bryce; not because he paid for everything, but because he cherished my presence. It meant a lot to him to be out with me and he showed me that, every time we spent time together.

Derek, on the other hand, just wanted someone on his arm. He wasn't charming. He never bought me flowers and, a couple of times, I even had to open my own door. Because we were both professionals and I made just as much as him, he viewed me as a complete equal and not a damsel-in-need. In his mind, I didn't need a 'Knight in Shining Armor,' because I was successful.

My degree could not comfort me at night. My paycheck did not tell me I was beautiful, and my car did not turn me on; I turned it on. There were so many other things I wanted Derek for but, because he couldn't see past my status, we couldn't make a commitment out of our casual dating. He was tall, fine, muscular, had a great sense of humor, and he was very poetic. I was very attracted to him physically and emotionally. Actually, he was a very stimulating man. He was just so damn cheap, and I got tired of being asked out on dates where I had to pull out my credit card. It was clear to me that this was a platonic friendship and not a courtship. I soon cut Derek loose because I didn't want to waste his time.

Derek is married now and his wife pays half of all the bills. I hope they make it work. (As an Update: before this book was able to make it to print, Derek and his wife split up; citing irreconcilable differences.) By his own admission to me, Derek said their differences was 99.9% over money.

Some people, both male and female, misconstrue the term independent. When I mention independence, I'm speaking of being self-sufficient. I don't think independently of a man when I am in a healthy relationship. I'm not in need of a man to pay my bills or to buy me things, because I feel as though if I can't buy it, myself, then I really don't need it. A woman, however, wants a man she can depend on; one who will be there to have her back when she just ain't got it.

Black men come into situations with instant radar thinking that if a woman *needs* him financially, she's a gold digger. You want all my lovin' and all of my time, but I can't call on you when times are rough and I need some assistance. You hear that whole 'I thought you were independent' speech and, once again, the communication gap causes a problem.

Men want to come to your house and eat your food, watch your television, drink all the beer, and expect you to give him a little somethin' somethin,' that night; *and* when you wake up in the morning. For what in return, dinner and a movie? My presence is worth more than all-you-can-eat at Sizzler or happy hour at Chevy's. Or better yet, he gets free tickets to a comedy show he didn't have to pay for because his homeboy works the door and he's got the hook up. Yet, we have to wait until the show starts before we can go in, and then we're sitting in some awful seats behind a pillar.

Women are becoming so self sufficient and/or independent that these same men, who refused to help her when she was down, now have their hands out because they need financial assistance. There is nothing wrong with being there for someone when they need it, but using someone because you know they have feelings for you is just wrong. Now I have to hear a tally of how much you spent on dinner and all the Madea plays I begged you to take me to.

So, who said it was politically correct for a black man to ask a single black mother for money? We all know about this jacked-up economy. Everyone is having financial problems, nowadays. It seems like those who had the most are hurting the most, right now.

I have this acquaintance; I'm not going to even say that we dated because, now that I look back, it seems as though our entire relationship was a joke. He was a very flashy type of guy; huge medallions, diamond watches, a drop-top Mercedes, etc. He portrayed the life of a baller, because everything he owned, you could see. It was tangible; no property, no lucrative business, just a bunch of materialistic B.S., by which he thought I should be impressed. First of all, my very first car, at sixteen, was a Mercedes. I went to private school and lived in a white affluent neighborhood. Our pediatrician was on the next block over, so all that "stuff" meant and still means nothing to me.

When he took a small step into my world and saw where I lived, where my parents lived, and what my life was about all of a sudden, he was in love with me. I couldn't have a conversation without him professing his undying affection towards me and, of course, I fell for it. Well, at first. I thought he was genuine but I soon realized it was just a ploy for him to get me to shell out cash at every opportunity he could find.

Sometimes your conscience tells you things, subconsciously. 'If it looks like a duck, walks like a duck, and quacks like a duck,' guess what, boo-boo? Chances are you are spending too much time with Donald Duck. Now I could have played the victim when I realized I was being used and not loved but, when I came to myself and knew who I was, I moved on.

I have never feared being alone. My fear is being in a situation with someone who is assigned to kill my purpose. If I feel shaky about you, then it's a wrap. If our courtship doesn't offer me security, what would marrying you do? I wish there was more evaluation than fornication in the dating phases. I wish I had come to all of these realizations before I had to live them. But then, had that been the case, there would be nothing for me to write about.

Ladies, if a man is dating you for what he can get out of you or from you, he is not dating you. Believe me, when a man is truly in love with a woman, he will do whatever he has to do to take care of her; not take from her. So, if he's taking from you, you can just believe he's giving to someone else; the one he's eventually going to leave you for. Please remember that. Stop telling these men what you have, how much you make, and stop parading around like you are 'Miss It,' when we all know you are struggling to keep the BMW, and the Gucci bag is a knock-off. If you pretend to have it, men will pretend to love you so they can get it, too. When your credit gets tarnished, he will bounce to his next victim. I'd rather be rich and pretend to be broke,-than to be broke and pretending to be rich. But then, that's just me. I had to learn that the hard way though.

CHAPTER 6

Black Men Have Given Up On Black Women

Sometimes I feel that because black men have ill relationships with their mothers, they now have it planted in their minds that all black women are manipulative and evil. I get so tired of hearing my African American sisters referred to as bitches and whores on a regular basis. I know everyone says this all the time, but we still keep hearing these derogatory descriptions of black women. It's on videos, it's in our movies, and now it's on the playgrounds, as well.

Now women, who pounce themselves up and down on poles for money and get half naked to be in a video, have brought it upon themselves to be disrespected that way. Even though it's not right and I still don't condone it, if you present yourself in a certain light to these men, they will address you in that manner. It's not what you are called, but what you answer to.

Will the Real Women Please Stand Up!

I was at a gas station filling up my car, when an old-school Impala with tinted windows, on 24s, pulled up to the tank across from me. I know we're not supposed to stereotype, but I was just ready for some ignorant, corn rolled, gold-tooth wearing, wannabe rap star to get out of the car and say something stupid. Dee Dub got out of the car and looked at me and said 'DAYUM MAH, YOU ALWAYS LOOK LIKE DAT?!' Huh?

With the radio cranked up past the level 10, his music was blaring so loud I could barely hear what he said. I just knew, however, that it was something real ghetto and ignorant. When I didn't reply, he called me a bitch. First of all, I couldn't hear him, because Too Short was hollering 'BIATCH' in the background from a pair of mounted sub-woofers that had my car shaking like an earthquake had erupted. Second of all, it was dark outside and he was so scary looking and, if I had even acknowledged his presence, he might have taken that as an invitation to start talking to me. Dee Dub went into the gas station to pay for his gas, then his friend, cousin, parole officer, or whoever he was, got out of the back seat and pretended to come over to pump the gas, when he really just wanted to talk to me.

He wasn't as ignorant as Dee Dub. He said, 'Hello, my name is Timothy, what's yours?' Dee Dub came out and was like 'Temo, don't even talk to that stuck up bitch. She think niggas out here broke or sumthin'. Timothy told me not to pay attention to him. 'He all liquored up and feisty.' Liquored up, but he just got out of the driver's seat. Wow. I get pulled over for a tail light being out, but here we have Dee Dub driving drunk and passing weed back and forth to Temo who, by the way, had just gotten out of jail. He'd been reading the last few months in Santa Rita, which probably explained why he was so calm and appeared educated.

The two other misfits sat in his back seat rocking as Timothy and I continued to talk for a few minutes. Meanwhile, as the gas pumped, Dee Dub got more and more irritated; mainly because he wasn't the one who got to converse. But, oh well, Timothy just happened to be at the pump. Dee Dub went in his car and came back with fliers, CDs, and all kinds of other promo stuff to show me who he was. And you know what? To this day, I still don't know. I don't know much about rap unless it's commercial, so I didn't act phased. To impress me, he pulled out a wad of money and started throwing it. I laughed as I got in my car and drove away.

So, this is how some black men with money act; they get angry because I don't respond to 'Dayum Mah' and then automatically assume I should get excited and change my mind because they throw money at me.

Dee Dub, just in case you're reading this, I had a wad of money in my purse, too, but I worked hard for it, so I'm not going to throw it at you to prove a moot point.

You'll see us on TV!' is what he said, as he skirted off from the gas station, leaving skid marks on the ground. I still haven't seen him or his entourage on TV but, then again, I don't watch *Cops* or *America's Most Wanted*. "Nah, Dee Dub, you'll see me on TV. I'll Holla."

So, there you have it. Black men have given up on us and don't know how to approach us in a respectful manner. The professional, proper English-speaking black men I come in contact with through business either view me as a threat or they want a white girl. So, I have to entertain the Dee Dubs, the Temos, and the June bugs of the world; the disrespectful, ghetto, black men who haven't a clue how to talk to me. But, when I choose to trade all that in for the affection of a white man, I'm viewed as a traitor. Therefore, I can date white men and deal with the backlash of other black people, deal with an uneducated black man who doesn't know how to communicate with me properly, or I can choose to remain single and go through this wonderful life alone.

CHAPTER 7

Black Men Don't Know What They Want

Men know what kind of car they want to drive, where they want to live, what college they want to attend, and all of the other major decisions that are made throughout the course of their lives. However, when it comes to choosing a woman, they seem to be so confused.

One minute, a man wants a woman who is independent and hardworking, but when he meets her, he is a little taken aback by her assertive personality. He soon finds out he can't control this woman, so he either cheats or moves on. He gives that classic line 'it's me, not you.' Then he wants the beautiful, Hollywood, model-type and, when he gets her, he tears her down until she doesn't feel beautiful anymore. The same pedestal that he put her on when they first met is the one he knocks her down from by making her feel no one else will want her. Then he wants the sweet, innocent, naïve, virgin, church girl and when he gets her, he cheats on her with every ho' from the hood because she's too prim and proper for him and not freaky enough. Why can't he make up his mind as to what it is he really wants?

Some men are confused and really want a mother figure in a woman but, at the same time, they expect her to be submissive. How can you expect me to fully submit to you when you are confused as to your role in the family? Some mothers have done a poor job raising their sons and, sadly, we are left with the unrealistic responsibility of turning them into the men we want them to be. Sometimes that can take a lifetime. If your mother took twenty years to ruin you, it would probably take another twenty to fix you. But the truth is, no matter how hard you try, you just cannot *fix* a man. The way he is when you meet him, is how he's going to be 5, 10, and 50 years later. He may evolve to be a better person for you, but "fixing" is just not part of the equation because he thinks he's just fine when you get him.

Personally, I'm not into fixing an emotionally damaged man. Once again, rather than deal with all of his childhood issues, such as the fact that his father was not around, and you (his mom) called him no good for all of his teenage years, I would just rather spend my time dealing with those men whose fathers taught them to go out hunting, fishing, buying stocks and bonds, and to provide for his family.

Now granted, I have had the looks and stares from white parents who wondered why their son was dating me, but this book is not about that; it's about choices; ones that women have.

We make the decision of whom we choose to deal with. There is absolutely nothing wrong with a black woman dating and marrying a white man, and there is nothing wrong with a black man dating and marrying a white woman. What became wrong to me is when black men started judging black women because of their decision to date white men.

What is wrong is when I see beautiful, educated, black women alone because black men are not interested, for whatever reason. We've had no other choice but to accept the Cuba Gooding Jrs., the Kobe Bryants, the Bryant Gumbles, the Tiger Woods', the Taye Diggs,' and all of the other successful black men we've seen squiring White women on their arms. We've had to bite our tongues while grinning and bearing it. Although it never really bothered me, it bothered a lot of sisters I know, and it probably still does. It's certainly these men's prerogative who they date, marry, and have children with, and the same should apply for us.

Don't judge black women for doing the very thing black men have done to us as soon as they found out they couldn't get lynched for it anymore. Now the tables are turned. We have so many beautiful options and black men can't stand it. Even black men who are with white women cannot stand to see a black woman with a white man. There is such a double standard among the sexes. To tell you the truth, I really don't care about society's double standards. I set my own standards and I live by my own rules. Whoever doesn't like it, can just dismiss themselves.

I hear black men say that black women talk too loud or too much, are bitter and angry, are not submissive, and blah, blah,

blah; "other" women are more accommodating to his needs and wants. I agree that some black women are assertive and aggressive, they roll their necks, point their fingers, tell you that you are not their father and they're grown, and all the other things they tend to say to prove their ultimate points. Well, if that's not the type of woman you want, then keep searching until you find a quiet, docile, submissive one, but don't discredit an entire group because the women in your family or neighborhood are loud and disrespectful.

You just may be looking in the wrong places. You grew up in the ghetto, your mom was on public assistance to feed you and your siblings and you have sisters who are still on assistance, as well. However, now that you are playing ball or have a good job, someone heard your song and you're an artist now, or you've been in two or three hit films, you have to get a white girl because girls from the "hood, where you grew up and learned the game, the same ones who loved you when no one knew you but your grandma and the social workers, are suddenly not good enough for you. They are too dark, too weaved, too needy, and too opinionated.

Black women come in all shapes, sizes, colors, and backgrounds. Some of us are privileged and some of us are poor. We have attended charm school (not Mo'Nique's) and Debutante balls, private school and public school. There are mixed girls with a variety of other races who make us who we are. There are so many different types of women to choose from but, because black men are not totally sure what they want, we get overlooked or passed by.

I am not being hypocritical when I say I have chosen white men over black, in some cases, when dating. It's not because I think they're better. It's because I think they are more available, more accessible, and more accommodating. I want my sisters to know that we now have the same choices these men have. Who cares if he overlooks you? Overlook him, right back.

It doesn't bother me one bit when I see a black man with a white woman because honestly, I am not even looking in his direction. If a good one comes along, who meets my qualifications, then I will eat my words. But until that happens and I am Mrs. "Somebody," my options will remain open to be with whoever treats me the way I was raised to be treated.

I have been told that I have chronic "princess syndrome." While I am not sure exactly what that means, I kinda have a clue as to what the premise is behind it. I have been there. I have tried to work with these men and they all have dropped the ball, at one point or another. Instead of slam dunking, the other team is stealing it and scoring.

Okay, let me shut it down right here. There are good black men out there. There are plenty of professional, hard working black men, some of which may be looking for an independent, smart, hard working black woman, like me. But, keep in mind, I live in California. Need I say more? There is a lack in the quality of black men on this side of the U.S. If you want a pants-sagging rapper who smokes marijuana and drinks Mickey's, then this is the place for you. However, that's not my type at all.

If you are into gay guys, then you'll hit the jackpot in California. They're not on the DL, out here. They are gay and proud in San Francisco. I do a lot of traveling and I love the East coast. In my opinion, the black men, out there, are more desirable, and have a lot more going on than the men on the West coast, but a lot of them are gay, too.

A difference can be found in D.C., B'more (Baltimore), Atlanta, and Houston, where many of the men are on the "down low." Their "gayness" is not accepted, so they date us and try to trick us. I can tell, *sometimes.* If, by chance, I meet a man who passes my "is he gay" test, I have to deal with the distance that separates us. I live in Cali, so a long distance relationship is what I have had to resort to in the past. After a while, that gets old.

Then again, we come back to the black man not knowing what he wants to do. Does he want to take this a step further and move out here, get married and start a family? Does he want me to pack up my life and move out there for him? If it's love, it shouldn't matter who moves where. That can all be worked out, but again these black men don't know what they want, whether it's out of fear or ignorance, so it still leaves me here to be pursued again by their white competitors.

Then we have the other extreme; those soft-punkish men who are sexually confused. While they're exploring and trying to decide what team they want to play on, they want to date a woman like me. Why? Because I have access to other handsome men they may want to get with? This lifestyle is common and, in my world of fashion, lights, camera, action, and event planning, it's hard to tell who's gay and who's straight. For this very reason, I am not into the Hollywood lifestyle beyond networking and business-relationship building. Although I am fond of one or two men in the industry, I'm afraid of the dangerous stories I've heard, firsthand, of the "boy parties" and bi-sexual activity.

If a man doesn't know if he wants a woman, he certainly doesn't know what type of woman he wants when a good one is staring him right in the face. Black men don't know if they want us to be thick or if they like us thin. Do you like weaves or would you prefer the short tapered look? Do you want us more aggressive or do you want us to submit? If black men weren't so vague as to what they wanted then, maybe, we could be all that they wanted us to be. We are so left in the dark by black men that we're not sure what we're supposed to be doing.

There was an interesting poll taken a while back in Essence Magazine that indicated that 66% of black men preferred black women. Where are these men? Not in the media, that's for sure. I support men like Will Smith and Denzel Washington who celebrate their Nubian queens and have battled to make their relationships work, when Hollywood is notorious for cheating for sport, couple swapping and failed marriages.

Once black men can define what it is they truly want from black women, if anything, then, perhaps, we can get together and create a harmonious atmosphere of marital bliss without drama. But, can that really happen?

We have been left in the dark for so long that, if we continue to wait for an indecisive black man, we will continue to be single when, in the end, all we really want is a family; a man who will step up and commit with his heart, his mind, and his body. If I could find that in a black man then, of course, I'd give him a chance; as long as he's not the likes of Dee Dub and/or Temo. Since it never seems to happen, that a grown ass black man wants a committed relationship with a black woman, I have come to the conclusion that marriage and commitment is not ultimately what they want.

CHAPTER 8

Black Men Mature Ten Years Behind Everyone Else

I love to hear Michael Baisden speak. He is also one of my favorite authors with his books *Never Satisfied*, *How and Why Men Cheat*; *Maintenance Man*; *It's Midnight, Do You Know Where Your Woman Is?*, and many others. Not only is he an award-winning author, in my opinion, he speaks the truth and doesn't make excuses for black men and their shortcomings.

Black women have done so well for themselves, at present, that if a black man has not stepped up his game and made a few accomplishments in his life, then he's left out in the cold. There is no excuse for a black man in his 30s to be still living with his parents. It doesn't even make sense, to me, for him to be renting. In today's society homeownership is a necessity. Renting is simply burning hard earned money every month, supporting someone else's real estate empire. But, of course, most black men don't realize that until their 40s and 50s. (***Disclaimer: I wrote this book at the height of the real estate game. There were constant, first-time homebuyer programs, at the time, and almost anyone with a full time job and decent FICO score could qualify at 100%. Today, that's not the case. Real estate has   plummeted and, for some, renting is a better option until the economy picks back up.***) Now, back to our regularly scheduled programming.

Black Women don't want a simple minded man. Even black women, who don't have college degrees, at some point, want their man to mentally challenge them. For a black man to challenge a black woman, he must first challenge himself. When I speak of a challenge, I'm not talking about being argumentative, but rather challenging to be better, to work harder and to achieve more. A "that'll do" mentality is plaguing our black men's psyche. If I'm striving for greatness, then why do I need you if you are fine just being mediocre?

We don't just want you to meet us where we are, but try to surpass us; not in a mind of constant competition, but to think as a provider. Black men find an accomplished woman with an education and they sit back and pat their bellies like they have arrived because black women, in the past, have become accustomed to taking care of them.

We, pretty much, follow music trends. Whatever is being played on the radio or shown on videos are the same things we see happening in real life. First, we had Mary J saying *"I can love you better than she can"* and women all over the world were competing with other women for their man. Then, in *"Enough Cryin'"* she said *"Don't wanna play house no more, so dumb to think you gonna marry me, I got to be out my mind to think I need someone to carry me….."* After that, women were saying "see 'ya" to the men who were stringing them along and not treating them right. Their mentality was, if Mary J said it, then there had to be some truth in it.

Face it, we are 35 years old now, and we have been dating each other for years. I'm ready to settle down with you and get married, but your 35-year-old, immature ass feels as though you're going to miss out on something, if you commit. A man knows, well before six months of dating, if you're the one or not. Most women know after the 2nd or 3rd date. Men want to make sure their friends give you the thumbs up and they want their family to like you, as well. A woman in love can care less if her mother or best friend likes you. 'If they love me, they will learn to love him,' is the way we think. Men are like teenage boys who have to be validated. If their boys don't like you, well then, something must be wrong with you. If their mothers think you're not the one then, clearly, you are not the one!

We all want our family and friends to get along with whomever we're dating and may ultimately decide to marry, but women don't base their relationships on what everyone else thinks.

Men put sex on the forefront of their relationships. They act like they want a respectable woman who they can chase, hunt, and prey but, if she withholds sex a second too long, his interests go in other directions. Women want the whole idea of intimacy before we even take it to the bedroom. Men, on the other hand, use love to get sex and women use sex to get love. There is a clear communication gap here. The maturity level has not been reached, yet, when a grown man feels the need to pressure a woman for sex. For most women that is a sure turnoff. When a man can't seem to think beyond his penis, it truly shows how mentally behind men are from women.

A man who will wait for you and commit to you, first, will make a better husband than one who just wants to get you in bed, right off the bat. I read an article in Ebony magazine where, once again, my favorite black man, Michael Baisden spoke out so profoundly." He said, 'Many men are lacking in three areas: 1) goals; 2) responsibility, and 3) integrity.' He goes on to say that there are men in their 40s and 50s who are habitual liars in their relationships. 'You cannot grow/mature without having the qualities of honesty, dependability, and integrity.' The last sentence hit me like a ton of bricks. 'If we were honest with ourselves, most men would admit that they are at least ten years behind where they should be.'

Wow, a black man said that; one who is an accomplished, successful, educated black man, at that. Why do black men find it so hard to be mature? These emotionally immature men make emotionally immature husbands, then emotionally immature fathers, and the cycle continues. If we get to the root of the problem, which is the fact that there are so many absent fathers in these men's lives, then we can work on equipping our youth to grow and mature at the proper pace to keep step with the rest of society. Something happens to African American males between the 2nd grade (8 years old) and 12th grade (18 years old) that causes them to mature slower. That ten-year gap puts them ten years behind, which is why it is no longer feasible for a man in his 20s to even think about being married, today.

The State of Black America (SOBA) report, an annual measurement on black progress, outlined these facts:

To date, a percentage of young black children are enrolled in early childhood education programs such as Head Start than young white children—66 percent compared to 64 percent," the report states. "And, the youngest blacks have made strong improvements in the areas of school readiness—scoring at 94 percent of that of whites, up from 81 percent in 2006." I believe, partially, it is because black mothers have to work and more white mothers are able to stay home with their children while their husband's work.

But, then something happens after elementary school as blacks— especially males—begin to fall behind whites.

Some of which they claim can be because of the following statistics:

- Black men are more than twice as likely to be unemployed as white men and make only 74 percent as much a year.
- Black men are more than six times as likely as white men to be incarcerated, and their average jail sentences tend to be 10 months longer than those of white men.
- At the end of 2001, 16.5 percent of the black male population had been to prison compared to 7.7 percent of Hispanic and 2.7 percent of white men.
- Young black males between the ages of 15 and 34 years are nine times more likely to be killed by firearms and nearly eight times as likely to suffer from AIDS.
- Of single parent black households, in 2005, only 12 percent were led by men.

- More than two-thirds of black children lived in one-parent households in 2005; the majority headed by women.
- More than 42 percent of black female-headed households with children were poor, compared to slightly more than nine percent of married black households.

So, while there are plenty of black men around that we can choose to deal with, we run the risk of being yet another statistic, and educated black women just don't want to take that risk. In order to get what we want in a black man, a black woman at the age of 25 has to date and marry a 40 year old man. Is that the state we are in today?

So many black men will be defensive about this, but look around. My co-author will have a chance to speak on your behalf, but it won't change the stats. It will not change the fact that America is looking at you, pointing the finger, and snickering. When a good black woman comes along, who sees your heart and your potential, you push her away.

Fear, ignorance, and pride will destroy our community. I surely don't want to see it happen, but I'm not going to tell my sisters to hold on and wait until a man turns 40 and is ready to settle down and marry them. I am going to tell my sisters to bid you farewell, put on some lip gloss, and put themselves in a position to be found by someone who deserves them. And don't be surprised if he's not black. A lot of men find us beautiful, even if our own don't.

CHAPTER 9

Successful Black Men Want White or Latina Women

The US post tells us that out of the 246,000 Black/White marriages that took place in 1992, more than half of those marriages were between black men and white women. Of course, that was 17 years ago. To date, these numbers have more than doubled. The further up the corporate ladder black men climb, the more we see them with a blonde haired, blue-eyed or Latina chick.

For many of our black men, particularly, our athletes, it has been set up. They aren't looked at as men, but as a franchise or some sort of commodity. I used to model and I got my start in the industry, first, as a promo model. Because of my drive, tenacity, and business sense, I knew that I wanted to be the person who hired the models and not the person doing the modeling, all the time. I wanted to be the business behind the beauty, so I started an event planning business.

It wasn't hard at all to land contracts, because I was already in the industry. Some of my major clients were liquor branding companies. I managed their sponsorship presence in Northern California. Wherever you saw Crown Royal, Tangueray, Skyy, or some of the other well-known brands, you would see me and an entourage of tall beautiful African American models promoting drink specials, hanging out in the VIP, and taking photos.

For more than five years, this is what my life consisted of and I must admit, it was a lot of fun. I started hosting after-parties for the Oakland Raiders, Golden State Warriors, and other Bay Area teams. I was never really into promoting myself; it was really all about my company, the product, and the models. This was an easy accomplishment because the players were hardly interested in any of us, even as beautiful as we all were.

I'm not much of a name dropper, but a certain person comes to mind when I think of successful, yet, immature men who make children but fail to commit. Maybe this would more suitable in another chapter, but the fact that he was so in love with a certain Latin mega-star, his name certainly comes to mind. I'm speaking, of course, of Sean Combs. Y'all call him P-Diddy, Puffy, or whatever name he's going by on any given week. He has three children with Kim Porter. Will they ever get married? My guess would be "no," because every three months he's dating someone else. He throws temper tantrums on national television, and the only talent he seems to have is finding gifted, impressionable, young people who don't read contracts or have the sense to hire their own personal lawyers.

Sorry to all you Diddy followers; I'm just not a fan. Also, I don't go with the flow of what everyone says is popular. I would rather do a crossword puzzle than watch one of his reality shows. He's my least favorite Hip-Hop personality in the public eye, and in my opinion, he's not the black man in the media to pattern one's self after, at all. I suppose his business savvy is keen enough, although he's more notoriously known for being a crook than a mogul. When it comes to his personal life, I find him to be despicable. Is he still dating Cassie or did Kim take him back *again?*

Black men seem to think that white and/or Latina women are more accommodating to their needs than black women. I say to you, Black man, we have gone through the same struggles that you have. We aren't trying to figure you out or understand what it's like to be black in America; we are black in America, too! We are discriminated against, judged, singled out, and overlooked, just like you. You're looking for someone to sympathize with you in your position, but we've been there, all along, with you.

We pulled ourselves up and black women seem to be able to move forward without blaming society, a little better than black men can. Some men feel as though it's a conquest or they are defying history by dating white women. Prior to the 60s, if a black man even looked improperly at a white woman, he could be and, often was lynched. So, given that history which has not been all that long ago, why are white women more desirable, now, than black women?

Latina women seem to always be focused on family. Their major goal in life is to be a supportive wife, mother, and nurturer. They don't seem to dream big outside of their neighborhood or close surroundings. Black men face no challenges, there. He can be the man and they're comfortable just letting him do that. They may work a job, here or there, but they'll never try to top or surpass their men. That isn't in their character or nature. Latina women are believed to be more submissive than their black counterpart. For a simple-minded black man who wants no challenges, this could be his perfect match.

One "D-list" actor, who shall remain nameless, once said that he 'was tired of waking up to his wife with a scarf on her head.' Now you know we, black women, will preserve our hairstyle, by any means necessary. You don't have that issue with white and Latina women since they wash their hair every day. Was this his reason for leaving his wife for a white woman? Because she wore a scarf to bed; was he serious? Though he's as black as the keys on my keyboard, he had something negative to say because his wife didn't just let her hair flow. I guess that's why I can say good riddance to black men who date white or Latina women. Their mentality is so off-balance that most of us don't want them, anyway.

CHAPTER 10

Black Men on the 'DL'

Although I briefly mentioned this before, for those of you who don't know, there is a vast segment of black men out there who are into this new alternative lifestyle called the "DL" or "Down Low." These are successful, educated, black men, who choose to engage in sexual activity with other men, yet do not consider themselves to be gay. They date beautiful women, get into committed relationships, and some go as far as to marry these women while, at the same time, they engage in sex with men, and the women in their lives are none the wiser.

I don't have a problem with a man who is just openly gay. You don't have to act like a flaming queen, but just be open and honest about your sexuality. I'm not going to judge you, but I will continue to stand on my soapbox and point the finger at these men who sleep with men and don't consider themselves gay or bisexual. These are the same men, who subject their families to the emotional and physical ailments that result from this reckless behavior.

As women, we look forward to the day when we will meet a decent man we can bring home to our family. We pray that things work out with him because in our hearts we believe he's "the one." After sifting through all of the jerks, dealing with one heartbreak and/or one let-down, after another, when we finally meet "Mr. Right," we know that our next step is marriage. It's almost as natural, to us, as breathing. Women don't want to date a man for 4, 5, or 10 years. If there is a connection, we want to make a commitment. Ultimately, we all want marriage and, when the timing is right, that is what we aim for. Now it's so unfair that we put so much time and effort into a man and then we come to find out that he's gay! Regardless, if you are dating or married to a woman and if you are having sex with a man, down-low or not, you are gay! You are also doubly wrong when you have a wife and engage in this behavior.

So, there you have it. Black women's choices are almost slim to none. Most desirable men are already spoken for and respectable women don't want to creep with unavailable men. Black men know have no clue what they want from us (i.e. mother, wife, bed buddy); Black men mature ten years behind everyone else; black men don't want to commit; successful black men want white or Latina women, and the lifestyle of those on "the DL" is taking over our community.

I don't want you to walk away from this book thinking that I have ill feelings towards all black men. That's not true at all. I love my brothers. The purpose of this book is to make black women aware that they have choices, and that it is okay to date white men or "other" nationalities.

For black men, it is to let you know what some women are thinking about you and, hopefully, you will step it up so our next generation has something positive to look up to. These are some of the things black women are saying about you behind your back: while you are walking around thinking you are God's gift to us all, we are laughing at you because you are ignorant; we want you to stop fathering children and not marrying their mothers; and, we want to be proud of you.

No longer will we pat you on the back or head and just say, "boys will be boys." That's why America's in the state that it is, now. We want to bring the black man back as the head of our households and work together as a unit. We aren't going to beg you to do what we all know is right and good. If you cannot meet our minimum standards, then we will continue to date your white counterpart. And, when you see us out together, don't point and get mad; just realize that you and/or your boys are not doing your job and you are leaving us with no other choices.

CHAPTER 11

LIPSTICK LESBIANS

Same sex relationships are certainly not new to us here in the U.S. We have accepted the fact that some people are gay. Whether the argument is that they were born that way or *became* that way is really not for us to decide or judge. What I have come to notice in my travels and meeting people from all walks of life, in particularly females, that some people have chosen this lifestyle because of their circumstances.

I know several women who, at one point in their lives, were married to a man and some even have had children in these relationships. One day, they had an epiphany that a man was really not what they wanted and they didn't need one to validate who they were. In some cases, these women have shared with me that they knew they were gay a long time ago. When they were in grade school, high school, and college, they were attracted to girls. Some experimented with females but they suppressed their urges and feelings because of the lack of comfort and support from family and friends.

But, a lot of the women I talked to and interviewed told me they were simply tired of men! They were tired of games, lies, cheating, abuse, emotionless sex, the lack of passion and romance, and the sense of being in a relationship and still feeling lonely. They felt the lack of communication drove them to forge closer relationships with their "girlfriends" while they both starved for affection. A lot of these women were in relationships with men or married to them and were having affairs with women. Sometimes, the other woman was married or in a relationship with a man, too. Most of these women didn't feel as though they were cheating on their significant other because they weren't sleeping with another man. Some chose to stay in their marriage or relationship with the man but received the affection and caressing from another woman who understood her and never made her feel as though intimacy was just for sex or a release.

A large portion of these women completely crossed over to the other side never to return again. They found everything they were looking for in a woman that they could never have 100% of, with a man. Women want someone they can talk to openly. They want someone who will understand what they're saying without always having to over-explain themselves. A woman does not want to be analyzed when she expresses herself. A strong and assertive woman also doesn't want to be viewed as weak when she has to release her emotions; when she feels the need to, sometimes, scream or cry.

I'm not sure why but, once a woman has achieved success, has a career, is financially secure, and things seem stable for her, men tend to think that she can't have a meltdown moment. This is something that other females are able to recognize. Therefore, they support one another.

Men seem to think that if they "put it on" a woman real good, he can have his way and do whatever he wants. If he is well endowed then, in his mind, she will be sprung for life. What a misconception! I know women who are turned on way more by a foot massage or a neck/back rub than they are by penetration.

Women are the most beautiful, delicate beings God ever created. While I love men and will always be attracted to the masculinity of a strong man, I find myself more understanding of why so many women have given up on the hope of finding their Knight in Shining Armor. Beyond physical protection, helping out with finances, and fertilizing an egg, many women are now viewing black men as liabilities they can do without.

A female can buy a gun for protection, work hard and have a roommate. She can use a vibrator and, if desired, can get artificially inseminated. So, why should she even take on the headache of dealing with a man? He won't commit to marriage. She can expect to get a yeast infection because he constantly wants sex, and, when he finds himself coming up short on finances, Ms. Corporate America, he expects you to pull out your wallet and come to the rescue.

I may have different views about this scenario, but this chapter is dedicated to my sisters who have given up on black men. I feel their pain and anguish, and my heart goes out to each and every one who has been hurt so much by a man that they can't even view him as a potential partner anymore. I can't help but wonder if some of these black women had considered dating or marrying someone other than a black man, would their present circumstances, yet, be the same?

CHAPTER 12

The Exception to the Rule

Now the media, news, law enforcement, and videos would have America believe that the men I speak of in this book are the *only* types of black men in America. This couldn't be further from the truth.

I'm a black woman so, naturally, I come from a black man. My father was a hardworking, retired veteran-turned-pastor and he always put his family first. I grew up on my little block, in my little circle, and thought all little brown girls had a dad like mine. It was my *naïveté* as I went into adulthood assuming that I would meet, fall in love, and marry a man just like my dad. I mean, all little girls who had my type of Bill Cosby-ish daddy wanted to grow up and meet their Prince Charming. I didn't grow up thinking he was non-existent, but he sure became hard to find.

I was always attracted to a certain type of guy; tall, caramel complexion, with a nice clean cut. As I entered college, I met a few and, by my own admission, sometimes I felt as though the boys I met in school were too nice or too boring. I was 19, fresh out of my parent's house and ready to *live;* whatever that meant, at the time. But, because of the school my parents chose for me to attend, I was surrounded by nerds, squares, and pastors' kids. I had just left an environment full of church boys and once I entered college, it was infested with them; too many pussy cats and not enough Dobermans.

As soon as I left college, I was determined to meet a rough neck; someone I was certain my mom would not approve of. He was going to be a man with tattoos, earrings and, maybe, even a record. Sounds dumb, I know, but it's the truth. In order for me to feel like an adult, I needed to shake that church-girl image and find someone who resembled the thugs I saw on videos; the ones I had to sneak and watch because of my parents' religious convictions.

Soon, just one short year after leaving Oral Roberts University in Tulsa, Oklahoma, I found myself dating my first rapper. He was tall, light, had braids, a gun, and an Iguana. I was so sprung because he was totally different from any guy I had ever met face to face. I mean, I saw guys like him on TV and in the movies but, to actually be out at Art's Crab Shack with this rough neck, it was an exhilarating rush for an innocent church-girl, like me.

I would leave Vallejo, on the daily, to sneak off to East Oakland to kick it with him. I sang on his demo tape, and hung out in the studio with him and his ghetto "partnas (sic)." We'd go to the lake and I'd sing along with the radio, while he was on the phone chit-chatting with his homies, customers, parole officer, or whomever. I was young, impressionable, and excited by this life I was introduced to.

I would go listen to him perform in the "hood" clubs of San Francisco while, all the time, my parents thought I was at choir rehearsal or some late night gospel musical. I was at a musical, alright; the infamous club Eddy, notoriously better known more for murders than music. What was I thinking, keeping time with this guy? He was the complete opposite of any guy I had ever been out with, but I suppose my youth was drawing me to him and I was just happy being a part of his little world, even if it was only during the weekends.

Our little "hip-hopera" would be short-lived, once it was time to move from the little cute side-kick who could sing to being his hood chick. I was 20 years old, a virgin and although, in my mind, I thought I was really a grown woman, I was still that naïve little church girl who was waiting for her husband, her Prince Charming; someone I could bring home to meet my parents. Yet, he couldn't come to the house for dinner. My outspoken mother would have never allowed it. So just as quickly as it started, that's just how quickly it ended; but not before I went to visit one of his hood spots because he had to take care of some *important* business. As he got out of the car (I had no idea where I was), he reached under his seat, placed a gun in my lap and said, "shoot first, ask questions later."

He jumped out of the car, hopped a fence and went into this little run down, brown house. I didn't know it then, but I know now, it was a drug house. He was dropping off his product and picking up some money to pay for his studio time and to fix up his ol' school Mustang.

I never knew a drug dealer, rapper, hood boy. While I was excited at first being engrossed into his rapper lifestyle, after that night, I never returned to Oakland again. Well, at least, not to see him. I stopped returning his messages on my pager and I tried to pretend I didn't like him, never met him, and never had that gun placed in my lap. What the hell was I thinking?

I was surrounded by good boys. It seemed like, in my age group, all the little church boys liked CiCi. I always got invited to movies, musicals (the church gospel versions), and to go bowling and, most of the time, it was fun. We would group date, so it would be like a dozen of us going to see the latest film or rolling gutter balls at the local bowling alley. I had to be home by midnight, which was cool because most of those nerdy boys did, too. I was back on my turf, my wavelength, doing what church kids do, and I was bored out of my mind. There were no rap concerts, tattoos parties, sideshows, dog pound, etc. I was going to see Commissioned perform in Sacramento, the Winans at Circle Star, and Lawrence Matthews and Friends at Good Samaritan COGIC in Oakland.

So, I was back in Oakland, but it was with a different crowd who had a totally different agenda. We were the church kids, the PKs, the misunderstood, the ones everybody thought was bad and up to no good. But we were good kids. Good kids who just wanted to have fun and enjoy life. I felt like life was passing me by, though. I was singing in community choirs and going to conventions from state to state. I was meeting other church kids from all over the country and singing in Memphis' Holy Convocation choir with Twinkie Clark and the late maestro and genius, Pastor Timothy Wright, but something in my psyche was telling me it wasn't enough. I wanted more.

I think I had stars in my eyes and I was searching more for lights, camera, and action than I was searching for Jesus, Jesus, and more Jesus. So, after the traveling, meeting up with my church friends from Jersey, Detroit, and Chicago, I found myself back in Oakland, again. This time I wasn't at a midnight musical with the local gospel singers and hanging out at Merits Bakery 'til 3a.m. Not this time.

I found myself another ghetto superstar; well, a barber, and I thought, this time, things would be different. He bought me flowers, took me to the movies, and I had my first glass of wine with him. At this point, I was fully grown, not living at home, and I was free to date as an adult. No coupled-up excursions like a Christian camp my parents, so often, opened up their home to. I was actually dating someone who saw me as a lady and treated me as such.

My nickname was 'boo,' lol! I had never had a nickname before and I thought it was cute, although, in the back of my mind, all I could hear was my mom chanting "don't be letting no snot-nose boy give you a pet name." As I thought to myself, *'what could she know. She'd been married to my dad since she was 18. She had never dated, so how could she advise me on dates and, for that matter, men.'* So I was 'boo' and he was 'sweetie,' and we went on our merry way.

I actually convinced him to visit church with me, one Sunday, and I think he liked it. And although he never went again, his mom and brother went with me a few times. I was in good with his family. He was a little hood and I was a little goody-goody. Together, we had a lot of fun, but the fact remained that I was still a naïve church girl who was ignorant to the ways of the world and men. I soon began to realize that I had bitten off more than I could chew. I was in over my head and the situation was suffocating me. I had let the boat drift too far off into the ocean and I needed someone to throw out a lifeline. I needed to get out.

Late nights of not coming home, always with the homies, not answering my pages and, all of a sudden, I was a bourgeois, spoiled brat and not the 'boo' he used to love. It was all an excuse; an excuse for him to be out doing whatever he wanted. I never questioned his whereabouts because he was all too quick to tell me where he was and to over-explain what he was doing.

Yes, I was young and impressionable, but I wasn't dumb. If your heart tells you something isn't right, chances are they aren't. I knew I wanted out of this relationship, but I think I was searching for a reason why. I explained that unhappiness wasn't good enough for me. I asked for a reason. I prayed for an escape. I wanted to get out and finally it happened. She called; the homie he had been spending all of his spare time with. Was I surprised? No. I had a pretty clear understanding of the guy I had allowed myself to love. Still, I was shocked. I was shocked that she had the nerve to call and tell me, she kept a calendar of all the times he was with her. I really didn't care. This was my way out and I took it. I walked away, never looked back and, basically, handed him to her on a tarnished silver platter.

This could have been my first experience where I could have been the instigator of black-on-black crime featuring black women. However, I have never been the type of woman who would sink to the low level of fighting over a man; especially, if he wasn't my husband. I took the high road, bowed out gracefully and went on with my life. On the other hand, he married her shortly after, and I couldn't help but wonder if something was wrong with me.

So, just like a teeter-totter, I went back. Every time the real world broke my heart, I ran back to my church world; my comfort zone. The people who had known me, since I was a little girl, understood my spiritual side. I never, once, stopped loving God or church. I just hated the formality and predictable course of organized religion. It seemed like everything I enjoyed and wanted to do was a sin. I couldn't even enjoy my life, a simple glass of white wine, or wear a nice pair of jeans without some hyper-religious person screaming that hell was enlarging itself.

So, as much as I tried to be back in the whole church life and dating a church boy, I still felt doomed. Doomed that, if I smiled too much or had too much fun, I would certainly go to hell. I also feared that, because I was now 22 and still not married, that I would be assumed an old maid, fast, loose or, even worse, a harlot. I was none of the above; just a misunderstood church girl who wanted someone to love her, unconditionally. I wanted someone who wasn't boring, a nerd, or a goody-goody, not like me. I wanted a nice, handsome, worldly boy who could teach me more than just what scriptures he learned in Sunday school, that past week.

I was so tired of the same-old, same-old and, because Vallejo had so little to offer a well-rounded, cultured girl like me, where did I find myself again? You guessed it; back in the melting pot of the Bay Area; Oakland.

It was there that I met someone who would change my life forever. Handsome, hardworking, outgoing, and not a church boy, but decent, nonetheless, he was not a rapper, street pharmacist, or any of those things I had encountered before in Oakland. He had a good job, a good head on his shoulder, he loved his mama, and he was infatuated with me. I could work with all of these assets. In my head, I planned a future with this guy. There was no one in my past that even came close to comparing with him. He was a nice guy with an edge; an edge because he lived in the "The Twomps;" a well-known area in Oakland. He was a nice guy because he respected me, opened my door, and courted me. I mean, he was from Oakland but he didn't act like the other Oakland boys I had encountered. For the first time I knew what it was like to be dating a man. He wasn't a man because of his age; it was because of his thought processes.

My nickname was 'Gorgeous' and, although his dad wasn't a pastor or Chief Adjutant to the Bishop (like my dad was), my parents loved him, nonetheless. That relationship, alone, made me change the way I viewed black men. Before him I thought all non-churched black men were ghetto, hood, and typical bad boys, while I remained with my notion that church boys were punks and too soft. It took him, 'Mr. Life Changer,' to make me realize that good black men come from all walks of life, all neighborhoods and backgrounds, and just because a man doesn't have a degree, it doesn't make him dumb. In my mind, he was one of the smartest men I had ever encountered. Although, sometimes when we argued, I called him "stupid" and stressed the fact that I went to college; oops my bad!

Seven years my senior, he taught me a lot about life, love, and commitment. He showed me what it means to support someone when you care about them. If it wasn't for him, I wouldn't be able to travel, do book tours, and be on the radio. When I'm away working and promoting myself, he's at home taking care of our son. So, there are exceptions to the rule; all black men don't make babies and leave them. All separated or divorced couples don't have to be angry and bitter towards each other, and a father can still be a father, no matter what the situation or circumstance is that surrounds his relationship with the mother.

As women, sometimes, we can control the situation. If we make our environment bitter and angry, we cannot then blame our men when they don't want to stop by and play family man for the weekend. We, as strong black women, have to learn how to manage our homes the same way we have learned to manage our jobs.

While there are still some men out there who are not going to act right, no matter what we do, in all honesty, most of them will do the right thing if we show them a little respect. So, instead of us jumping on the band wagon with the media, the news, and law enforcement, and agreeing that all black men are bad, scarce, invisible, ignorant, and–baby makers, let us agree that there are a lot of good ones out there. And just because a guy is nice and doesn't sell drugs or calls us a bitch, it doesn't mean he's a punk, a sissy, or boring. It simply means he was raised right. Whether it was a by single mother, his grandmother, or his parents happened to be married, a black man will give you what you give him.

So, instead of us always looking for a baller, shot caller, or industry groupie, who can get us in all the hot after-parties and the VIP sections of the clubs, we need to set our affections on the UPS man, the cable guy, the bus driver, the postal worker, the security guard, and the maintenance man. While many of them don't have degrees, they are still good men and the majority of black women have been overlooking them because they aren't manicured and driving Mercedes-Benzes.

If a black man marries you and you already have a Mercedes, then you both have a Benz. But, if you pass him by because his annual salary does not match yours, then you'll be opening the door of luxury by yourself. Maybe, when we look past his bank account and look into his heart and the fact that he can love us just as well, the stats won't indicate "70% single." Perhaps, they'll eventually show that just 50% of us are single. While that percentage would still be considered "high," nevertheless, it's a start.

CHAPTER 13

Blame it on the Rain

Remember that 80s group, Milli Vanilli? They were the two pretty, brown boys with dreads from Europe, who completely took over the airwaves and videos with their hot single, "Blame it on the Rain." While I vaguely remember some of the lyrics, I do remember a portion of the song saying *'whatever you do, don't put the blame on you'* .... *'you gotta blame it on something......'* blah, blah, blah! The song was entertaining and cute, but their celebrity status came to a screeching halt when the world found out the deceiving duo was "lip-synching" because they really couldn't sing; surprise, surprise, surprise! I would imagine such a scandal would have been a big deal in the 80s when so many artists "could" sing as opposed to how surprising it is, if an artist in today's music industry *"can"* actually sing.

So now, let's skip ahead 20 years later to Jamie Foxx; one of the most talented personas in entertainment, when it comes to comedy, movies and music. I will stop what I'm doing whenever Jamie's on the radio or television. I loved him in the movies *Ray*, *Ali*, *Dreamgirls*, and *The Soloist*. No matter how many Oscars he wins, I will never forget the day I heard the single from his *Intuition* album and started immediately blasting it on my CD player at home, the radio in the car, and I even downloaded the ring tone.

Okay, I'm a Jamie Foxx fan, so sue me. The song I'm referring to, that has been the hottest song in the club and gets repeated requests several times in any one given night, is: you guessed it; "*Blame It*." So, whatever mess you end up in that night, after you leave the spot, if you have to blame it on something, 'just blame it on the alcohol.' Ha! I love it! But now it's about to prove my point.

When it comes to male and female relationships, and I specifically speak on black relationships because, believe it or not, I'm a black girl no matter what I check on census forms, there is always something to be said about the way we communicate with one another. We all know that women are better communicators, (or we communicate more), which is not a black or white issue. We admit that, sometimes, we are too emotional and, sometimes, we just want you to listen and, oftentimes, we choose the wrong time to want you to listen (i.e., you are on your way to work, the game is on, or your homie is on the phone), but we feel it is of the utmost importance that our point is made; even if most of the time there is no point. All we want is for you to listen to us.

So while I spent day and night compiling my thoughts, ideas, experiences, and questionnaires for this book, I got into a few heated debates and arguments about the subject. It wasn't just about what I was writing, but how I portrayed black men.

The African American family is slowly being destroyed and, honestly, I'm not sure if many people are paying attention or if many of them care, for that matter. America, as a whole, may not give two wooden nickels as to what's happening to us but I, for one, care about the plight of my son, my family, and my community. I have come to a point in my life where it's not about just me and mine; it's about us, and that's whoever "us" is to you.

As I went on with a few of my male friends on how I view our relationships, our families and our men, one of my boys (we'll call him Semaj) began to point out some keen facts; not about women as a whole but about me, my   personal choices and how it relates to women as a whole. He has known me since I was a teenager, so he knew about my fascination with bad boys, rough necks, and wannabe rappers, etc. He also knew that I thought square boys and pastors' kids were boring, and I wanted tattoos and bad attitudes.

As I began to examine how I was when I was in my early 20s and how it related to me, now, as a young woman in her 30s, with a male child and, now, having the audacity to want a "nice guy" or a "square" by definition, I clearly sent mix messages to men. Am I the only one?

Have black women disregarded the average nice guy for so long that we have turned him into the rough-neck that we say we, now, don't want? Like the boys from private school trying to act hard because they wanted to impress the ladies only to find out that once they crossed over, the ladies really didn't want them anymore. Have we gone as far as to try and teach our sons to be hard and insensitive so they won't be viewed as punks and, now, that they are adult men, women don't want them because they are emotionally immature?

Some of the same guys I enjoyed spending time with when I was 21 and 22 years old, hanging out in Oakland, are the very guys I don't want hanging around me or my son, now that I'm 30+ and thinking about a family.

So, since it's said that good girls like bad boys, have we spent so much time giving them all of our attention that we don't recognize the good ones; the diamonds in the rough, and the roses grown from the concrete? Black men care about family and connection as much as women do. They form gangs. Why? They do it to establish a sense of family. They join motorcycle clubs. Why? It's their way of having some sort of brotherhood outside of the "frat family" that college boys join.

Because I have learned to stop blaming, I noticed that, in many circumstances, black women have contributed to the absence of the men in our lives. In one way or another, we have run them off because of our outlandish demands, our wants coming before our needs and, sometimes, because of pure selfishness.

We tell our men that we want them to go out and work hard so we can have everything we see our girlfriends with but, if they are gone one hour too long, we complain that they're never home and we threaten to leave or some resort to cheating. I think sometimes we send the wrong message to our men when we claim to be confused when it comes to whether or not they want us to be independent or to need them. They know if we want them around all the time or if we want them to work around the clock so we can have the nice dishes in the cupboard. Our flakey nature has driven a lot of them away and, so the fact that we out-number them becomes even more evident due to the fact that the ones we do have access to, we throw away.

So, now, we have climbed this coveted corporate ladder and have this life that most people envy but, while on the outside looking in, we have become what some deem as successful and we're still alone.

We haven't learned how to balance wife, mom, career woman, and business owner. We think that getting married and being submissive makes us weak after we have spent eight or more years in college and run things every day at work. Since we have adapted the "I'm like Oprah and I don't need a husband either" attitude, our men are not marrying us. It isn't because they don't necessarily want to be married, but they don't want to commit to what can possibly be a life sentence of all the trials and tribulations we have faced with men in the past. It's that attitude they get from some of us because we have that expensive degree and a house in a middle-class American neighborhood. Do wives, who make more money, fully submit to their husbands?

While I do believe there are a few black men out there who cannot and will not meet us halfway, I also believe that there are a lot of black men out there who want us, love us, and are waiting on us to show them that we want them, too. A relationship is definitely a two-way street and it takes two people to make it work.

While I still feel as though black women have choices and should be able to choose whatever men they believe will make them happy, I will admit that we have contributed more to the problems we have with black men than we have in actually coming up with workable resolutions. For the sake of the black family, I am willing to work towards being a part of that solution but, at the same time, I will continue to leave my options open to love whomever will love me back and love me right.

Instead of blaming now, which is what I have done most of my young adult life, I have decided to talk about it. I think it's important to lay all feelings out there on the table so some black men, who are slightly interested in how we feel, may decide to open a dialogue with us. I have argued enough in my life. I don't want to argue anymore. I want to converse, discuss, and talk about the things that separate us. I don't want our men to be viewed as thugs, jail birds and drug dealers, just as I don't want our women to be viewed as pole ornaments, loud, uneducated, non-supportive, and gold-diggers.

The only way we can get past those stereotypes and create harmony among ourselves is to open up the lines of communication and be completely honest about our feelings. If we can't be open and honest with ourselves, how can we expect the rest of America to listen to us?

So, black men, are you going to take heed to the message so we can move forward or will you be offended by my frankness and continue to blame? I've admitted my faults and shortcomings and, in all fairness, will you admit to yours as it relates to me, a black woman?

CHAPTER 14

written by Marlon Green

The Black Man's Rebuttal

When it comes to comparing black men with white men, the woman doing so must ask herself, "Am I running from black men and running to white men?" "Am I curious about white men, or merely exploring my options?" Whichever the case may be, please be open and honest with yourself. Do not, under any circumstances, allow one-sided, biased opinions and irrelevant, non-conclusive data to influence you. As great as black men are, do not allow the ugliness of weeds to overshadow your vision of the roses available.

When it comes to the art of degrading black men, other than the news, poor statistics are always the source used to create negative views and to manipulate public opinion. They will state that there are more black men in jail than in college. In reality, all studies show that, in the college age range of 18-24, there are more black men in college than incarcerated at a 3:1 ratio. Hearing it put that way is much easier to understand, more relaxing to the mind, and promotes hope and optimism for a brighter future.

Statistics can be very helpful and insightful, but they can severely impair and fatally damage the mind, if interpreted negatively. The same statistics that show there are three black men in college to every black man incarcerated also show us there are more black men in jail than incarcerated. How can that be? Well, the ages of all black men in jail span from 18-years old to those well into their 70s, while the ages of college students span from 18-24-year olds. That study is parallel to the statistic that shows there is a despairingly wide gap between dogs in the pound (jail) than in dog training school (college). That is because dogs can be in the pound from birth until the twilight years (from 7 and beyond), while dog training is generally from 8-weeks to 11-months old. Take the amount of dogs in the pound between the ages of 8-weeks old to 11-months old, and compare it with those of the same age in training school, and the gap decreases drastically. The same applies to black men in college versus black men in jail; there are more in college.

My lovely co-author paints a picture of black men that drop out of college and become low-paid, bitter, violence-prone men that look to leach off women; thus, they can only be seen by black women as being charity cases when it comes to marriage. However, any woman that prefers a college-educated man should dive into the pool of, according to the statistics given, over 160,000 black men graduating from college every year. Out of 160,000 graduates, I truly hope a good woman is capable of building a healthy relationship with at least 1. If not, her goals, motives, and methods must be questioned and revamped.

The bookends of the college versus jail debate unfortunately leaves out a crucial piece to the three-piece puzzle — the black men who do not attend college nor go to jail, but are educated and lead productive lives. It is essential to note that many millionaires never stepped onto a campus, but they did study, learn, and eventually specialized in a particular skill or service. Today's society continues to blossom with black men that took the entrepreneur route and became successful; many outpacing college graduates of any race. In addition to the entrepreneurs, there are millions of men in the military or working as mailmen, firemen, plumbers, policemen, trash men, electricians, etc., all of which make more money than school teachers, which, by the way, have college degrees and often master degrees.

Graduating from college does not ensure progress in the workplace nor in finances. Attaining a college degree simply means that a person passed a series of assignments and tests, and met the institution's criteria. It doesn't mean the graduate will get a job, and if the graduate does get a job, it doesn't mean the graduate will receive enough money to his standards or the standards of others. Furthermore, a degree will not ensure that the graduate will keep his job. A college degree is not worth the paper it is printed on. The degree is useless. The only value and power a graduate has is applying the knowledge he received.

Black women, having a man that has a college degree will not lead you to happiness. There are many traits, characteristics, and socio-personal intangibles that should have much more importance on your list of wants in a man.

What must you do to get a black man to commit? There is absolutely nothing you can do. Every man must want to be committed to a woman on his own accord. A woman's wonderful personality, beautiful appearance, great sex, nor large bank account cannot make a man commit.

A major problem in this equation is women who do not honestly let men know what they want. You must establish your wants, needs, and expectations from the onset and ask him his.

Black men have not mastered the art of non-committal relationships, but they have taken advantage of the free samples being offered by women that are lonely, competitive, have low self-esteem, and are naïve, hurt, obsessive, possessive, or shallow. No matter the race nor gender, some people will take advantage of situations that lean in their favor.

As times have changed, so have the roles of the genders. Women are becoming stronger and more powerful, and with that strength comes the power to make choices — including sleeping with a man on the first date. The independent woman's burden is she wants to act like a man, be treated equal to a man, and then choose when she wants to be treated like a woman. That mental instability causes too much confusion in relationships and will almost always be their downfall. Women need to be themselves, play their position, and accept the drama and heartbreak that come their way when they do not.

When it comes to a man shacking with a woman, that is a form of commitment. He is committing his finances, time, and space to that woman. Maybe it was the woman's idea to try on the shoes before buying them, or maybe she needed help with the bills in this terrible economy. Shacking can be a great thing, and maybe it was the woman who came up with the great idea to shack.

Now regarding the Black men that want to be married but are hesitant and taking their time, it is because they want to be sure they are making the right decision with the right person at the right time with the right circumstances. I took that route because I wanted to be the best husband I could be to the woman that I wanted to be with *forever*. Forever is a long time, especially when you make a mistake and choose the wrong woman. Why buy the milk *when the milk can go bad?* Black men do not fear the possibility of failing at marriage, but rather failing to choose the right woman.

Cream rises, so those women who want to be married should be themselves, stick to their morals and standards, and be the ultimate complement to the type of man they want. If marriage is a woman's ultimate goal then she should act like it all of the time and only invest time, effort, and emotion in men that want to be married and value it as she does.

Marriage is not for everybody. Like some black women, some black men simply do not want to get married. They may have thought it over for years and decided against it. They may have witnessed abusive relationships, have trust issues, they may be selfish, or maybe they are career oriented or simply loners. Not wanting to be married is not to be looked down upon. Marriage is a choice, and some people choose against it.

Some men plan not to be married until a certain age (some wish to wait until they are beyond 30), while some wish to wait until they achieve a certain status of education, wealth, and/or property. In both of these situations you will find great men that want to be married, however, marriage is out of the question at the present time. Women may chalk them up as players, noncommittal, womanizers, or having cold feet, but they are simply disciplined men with solid goals.

Black men see black marriages flourish and prosper, and they know about commitment, but many do not see any value in commitment due to women being attracted to superficial things. It appears that women flock to athletes, entertainers, gangsters/thugs, money, jewelry, and cars, so, like the women, the average man throws intangibles like integrity, honesty, morals, and commitment out of the window and seeks the superficial items that attract attention. The good women, along with the women that suddenly change, find themselves in the presence of men ill-equipped for healthy relationships. If you want to find a good black man among the masses, see beyond the glamorous front and peer into the actual man. Those without substance cannot put up a façade for long. Once you recognize someone as being something other than what you are looking for then move on immediately. Don't leave the door open for casual sex, someone to call when you are lonely, or booty calls.

If the men you all are dealing with are not men then don't sleep with them, don't have a child by them, and, better yet, beyond telling them about themselves, don't bother giving them the time of day. If you are caught in an unfortunate situation with a man that you don't respect and cannot be proud of then you are to blame for your decision to be around him, having sex with him, and conceiving a child with him. You have total control over your actions, so act wisely.

Women are 100% responsible for having children out of wedlock with irresponsible men. Women have the power to not have sex, to not be controlled by their hormones, to not be sweet-talked, and to not be placed in a position they don't want. When it comes to abortion, I always hear chants of *pro-choice* — does pro-choice not include a woman's right to not have sex? Does pro-choice not include a woman's right to choose whom she wishes to have sex with? Every time a woman lies down with a man, she takes the risk of becoming pregnant. Women commit an injustice to themselves if they want to be married before becoming pregnant, but still become pregnant.   If she wants a man that will be a role model for their son then carefully find and marry that role model before having a son.

I, along with many other men and women, have never faced the embarrassment of enrolling a child in kindergarten with a last name different than ours because we either chose or were careful enough not to have a child before marriage.

Ask me, "Who said it was okay to father a child and not marry the mother?" and I'll ask, "Who said it was okay to have a baby by a man you are not married to?" All black women should exercise their better judgment when it comes to finding an eligible mate to avoid having to raise their sons and daughters alone. Young women mimic the actions of the irresponsible, sexually active women they see. Single parent families are beyond epidemic, they are now a way of life.

Regardless of the situation, there is never an excuse for a man not to raise and support his offspring. Even if the mother is vindictive or spiteful, the children should be taken care of to the fullest without the urging of family court. But beyond mere child support payments, only a man can teach a boy how to be a man. A woman can only try. The solution is to find a man that is willing to teach and raise a son before having a son. It is a travesty when the child does not grow up learning how to love a woman because there is no father present to love his mother, and an equal tragedy is a daughter growing up without learning how she is to be loved properly.

CHAPTER 15

written by Marlon Green

Who Says Black Men Are Not Faithful?

The notion that Black men are not faithful is a false statement that often lands many women in trouble in their relationships. The second you buy into the untruth of us all being unfaithful is when you have completely given up on love and having a monogamous relationship. Thankfully, I never submitted to the false notion that it is a man's nature to cheat or the false notion that it is acceptable behavior.

Men act in accordance with their value systems. I am a married man, and three of my closest friends are married — none of us have cheated on our wives. Not only were we prepared for marriage before making the decision to be married, but our value systems contained committing to love, trust, loyalty, patience, communication, teamwork, monogamy, and responsibility. Are we special men? No, but we may be deemed special by some because we seem to be hard to find. However, we are normally right under your noses, but remain unseen and passed over by women with their priorities and values in the wrong places.

As for the Black men who are unfaithful, there are many reasons other than those mentioned, but I will cover hers first. Too often men use cheating as a scapegoat. Truthfully, a cheating man who either wants to continue to get away with cheating or refuses to look in the mirror will use any reason for his infidelity that the women will give credence to. It is normally about a woman's weight and more about his desire for variety. However, women need to stop using their weight or their offspring as excuses. Keep in mind that overweight women can be more attractive than women with the "perfect weight" who do not take good care of their appearance. Moreover, not all women that have been married for years have kids, so who is to blame for their weight gain? And for those that have gained after having a child, losing weight starts with changing your eating habits, shopping habits, consistent exercise, and changing your lifestyle. Men are bothered when they see a woman with three kids in perfect shape, while their wife with no child or one child is unable to stay out of fast food drive-thru lines.

And what is this about women losing their sexual appetites after having children? What about the women who ration sex, a month after the wedding? What about the women that do not have any children but still withhold sex? What about the women that have older children but still refrain from sex? There are two things to note: 1) - the women that allegedly lose their sexual appetites may have had an artificial sexual appetite just to get that man; 2) - the women may not have lost their appetites at all, they are simply not motivated to have sex with the men they are with. Present a woman with the hypothetical question of making love to her favorite singer, actor, or athlete and she will feel an immediate surge in sexually-urged hormones.

Men don't cheat due to women not satisfying their sexual fantasies, but they may cheat due to women satisfying their sexual fantasies and then stopping abruptly. Today's women are said to be sexually liberated, in tune with their bodies, and far more advanced sexually than men. With that being the case, along with their sex drives, there should be no restrictions in the bedroom that were once permitted.

In reality, many women use their weight, alleged lack of sexual appetite, and not wanting to do certain sexual acts as power to control men. Unfortunately, power used inappropriately eventually produces undesired results.

My major reason for black men being unfaithful is as follows — take the boy/young man that is taught that since he is young that it is best that he plays the field until he gets older, gets an education, or a good job. By the time any of these occurrences take place, the boy/young man is conditioned to not settle down. Taking a 25-year old man and expecting him to suddenly take on new relationship habits is like placing a lawyer in an operating room to perform brain surgery. Men genuinely do what they have practiced doing up till that point of their lives. They are what they practice. If a boy/young man has practiced playing the field, then he will only get better at it as he ages.

Simultaneously, girls/young women are often taught to not get into any serious relationships or not to deal with men and concentrate on their education. These women may be under the assumption that when they finish working on their careers they will find Mr. Right according to soap operas, movies, and love songs. The reality is they achieve their degrees and get into relationships with their male counterparts and a "collision" takes place because these women have no practice or experience in working toward and building a relationship with a man. The only experience he has is in playing the field, hunting women, and engaging in behaviors that are not conducive to relationships. Neither have experience with relationships, they don't know how to work together, and they don't know their roles, all of which influence being faithful to your partner or spouse, so these relationships either quickly falter or struggle to avoid the inevitable.

Other than the conditioning of American pop culture, other reasons for cheating include it being in a man's nature, greed, lust, ego, boredom, the expression of pain, a weak support group, not knowing how to say no, and the other woman, but all of those are copouts. If a man has issues or weaknesses in any of those areas, then it needs to be worked on before he takes on the seriousness of being in a relationship.

The fact of the matter is this, men that cheat, just like the men that are faithful, make a choice. Regardless of how they feel, where they are, and who is presenting them with an opportunity, men have the power to reject an affair or accept and indulge in an affair. Cheating is a choice made by the man, not inherently by his biology or any other frivolous reason.

Many "successful" women think they have a problem finding a man because men cannot see beyond their status, but the truth of the matter is most of those women cannot see beyond their own status. A professional woman's demise will begin the minute she equates a good man with a salary that must adjust to hers, if necessary. Men and women fall victim to money woes when they have money and when they don't.

If there is a happy couple with a man making $50,000, and the woman making $40,000, why should the woman allow her job advancement or new job, which pays $60,000, to change the dynamics of her happy home? If she is being paid $100,000, then the difference in their salaries is even wider, but her man has not changed. He is still the same man she was happily in love with before her new salary, but she has allowed her salary to change the dynamics of her personal life. Even worse, if she suggests, encourages, or demands that her man makes at least $60,000, then she is creating a salary comparison or competition by herself.

For the women that understand how love works and choose to control their relationships rather than allow money to control them — wonderful. But for the women that are controlled by money, you are hindering your own happiness and making yourselves unavailable to many men that wish to enhance your lives and your success.

And what happens to the woman that gets that pay raise, stresses her man or leaves him, and then gets laid off or fired? Does she then learn that a job title and a salary are not what make her? What if she cannot find employment that offers a higher salary than the one she had before she became "successful?" Does she honestly find a man to love or does she find a man to suit her for her current salary?

Regarding who pays what household bills and what percentage, each household operates under its own guidelines, which should be laid out from the onset. However, a woman should not allow the payment of a bill to obstruct her happiness, and a professional woman should not have a problem paying half of the household bills because she would realize his salary subsidizes half of the entire bills. Before becoming one with him, she was paying 100%. Now she has a problem paying half of what she previously paid all of? How much sense does that make? The two are to become one unit, not two separate entities under one roof. Your money is supposed to work together.

Women in general are torn between traditional and modern values, and the travesty becomes worse when they pick and choose when they want to adhere to one set of values over another.

As for your Bryce-Derek analogy, Bryce was looking for marriage, while Derek was looking for sex. The solution is simple: find a Derek that is looking for marriage. It should take more to impress you than a man picking up the bill. If your beliefs say the gateway to finding a good man is his ability to spend on you, then you are setting yourself up to be bought, misguided, and heart-broken. A man can cherish your presence without spending a dime.

The Dereks of the world are often overlooked due to false perceptions and baseless comparisons. You thought Derek just wanted someone on his arm, but he wanted someone to work with as a cohesive unit in marriage. His wife probably thanks God everyday that so many women with superficially-twisted values sabotaged their happiness and passed up her knight in shining armor. Congratulations to the women that married the Dereks of the world.

A generally accepted point of view of black women is that black men are intimidated by independent, hardworking women. I have never been intimidated by those qualities in a black woman, and there is nothing unique about my sentiments because most men are not intimidated by those qualities. When those women that wear their "successes" or "achievements" on their sleeves as badges of honors, which include salaries, job titles, the amount of the home they own, and the amount paid for vehicles, they can easily drive men away. They are not intimidated, but they are tired of female egos, superficial values, bravado, facades of strength, etc.

Some women take independency too far. My mother is very strong and independent, but when I was in college, she warned me of dealing with women who were *too independent* because they unnecessarily fight, debate, create dramatic situations, and operate to where the relationship goes in two different directions. Her words still ring true as I meet countless single women and women struggling for power in relationships. Too much independency puts out a message to the universe that you want to be alone.

What kind of women do men want? Realistically, we want a woman that is attractive and in shape according to our individual standards, knows how to cater to and tend to our needs and desires, is a very good friend that we can trust and will trust us, knows how to cook, never nags, and knows how to take care of home.

Idealistically, we want a woman that is very attractive and in shape according to our individual standards, but also has the ability to transform herself into other looks almost to the point where she can be looked upon as a different woman. We want a woman that has little to no sexual partners, but is the most experienced lover in the world. We want a woman that can cook when we are hungry, talk when we want stimulating conversation, and know how to close her mouth when it is time. We want a woman to always be at her best, never do anything that will turn us off or take away from her feminine wiles. We want a woman to be aggressive when needed, neutral when needed, and submissive when the situation calls for it. In short, we all want Claire Huxtable.

Are you confused, ladies? Although we want too much idealistically, many of those characteristics can be found in the right woman. Ladies, if you are having trouble finding a man then you probably are falling short in most of the areas mentioned in both the realistic woman and idealistic woman categories. Instead of constantly lacking or insisting one takes you as you are, how about becoming the best woman you can be? How about bringing more to the table? I told my wife that I would have married her after the first 30 days of knowing her and I meant it because she brought all but one of the characteristics of the combined categories to the table. I did not ask that of her, I just recognized it when it came along and wasted no time doing anything outside of building a strong friendship and relationship with her. You are reading the words of a man that has not and will not cheat.

Now when it comes to the maturity of a black man, if he has a plan and he's in the process of implementing it then there is absolutely nothing wrong with him living with his parents. I know a few who paid for college, cars, and a fully furnished home after staying with their parents. Ladies, what is more attractive than a man that knows how to make money work and a man that does not have a mortgage or car note?

And if a man lives in his own apartment, then open your mind to him possibly being great with money, having no debt, and a high credit score, but he prefers not to buy a home or has not found the right place. Owning is not for everyone. Ask the hundreds of thousands of people who are facing foreclosure, have been foreclosed on, or are struggling from paycheck to paycheck because they are house poor.

Unlike my brilliant co-author, I feel a man should not try to surpass a woman because a relationship is not a competition. And what a man finds happiness in may be considered mediocre to some women, but successful to others. Progress is subjective. Ladies, if you want a man that aspires to be a mogul, a mover and a shaker, and a heavy hitter in the corporate or business world, then seek that quality from the beginning. By no means should you destroy what is or can become a great relationship because you feel a man that is doing well can do much more according to your personal standards.

You want to know a hidden practice of immaturity? Withholding sex. Why, because withholding sex is selfish, and being selfish is so immature. Sex should be used as a form of expression of love and sharing of emotions, not as a weapon of control. And it is perfectly fine to wait until you marry Mike before having sex with him, but during that period it is not fair to have sex with Kenny while continuing to pass yourself off to Mike as saving yourself for him. And then there are women that have sex in high school, college, and after college, but when they find 'Mr. Right' and get engaged, then they want to abstain from having sex until after the wedding. How backwards is that for women in their 20s and 30s?

Basically, in order for a black woman to get what she wants from a black man at the age of 25, she has to have her act straight, be free of playing mind games, emotional games, and sex games, know what she wants in a man, and not settle or invest her time in men that possess qualities other than those she wants in a man. If she finds a man that she has a clear communication gap with, then she needs to find a man that "speaks her language," whether it be monogamy, marriage, salary requirements, physical characteristics, family values, etc.

I never dated anything other than black women, so those black men who have will have to make an argument in support of their decision of choosing a Latino, Asian, or White woman. Do not be swayed by the decisions of popular men who have gone that route. We often see a cluster of celebrities that choose Latino, Asian, or White and assume it is considered the thing to do, but it's not.

There is absolutely no reason for a man to mislead a woman and present his sexuality to be something other than what it is. However, if a woman doesn't want a gay or bisexual man, learn about him before getting involved. It usually only takes a little time to realize a man is gay, bisexual or if he is what you want, in general. Many women choose to have a man over putting in work to find the right man, so they end up turning a blind eye to unwanted truths about that man. You must love yourself enough to accept the best.

Black women have plenty of good black men to choose from. They simply have to choose the men they plan to spend the rest of their lives with, with the same thought, fervor, and precision they put into purchasing a pair of shoes. The amount of newlyweds and young, happy brides is evident that desirable black men are available. Black women need to always remember that all of the good men that are taken were once single.

Despite the many shortcomings of white men, I didn't put them down while stating the case and shedding light on black men. Let it be known that buying into the notion that white men are rich, have good credit, and know his role in the family is a quick way to put yourself in danger.

White stereotypes do not ring true. If you find a white man that takes care of everything, it simply means *that* white man has money or access to it. It doesn't mean that all white men have money. Even when it appears he is wealthy, that may not be the case. He may be running up credit cards, home equity loans, or doing something else regressive to barely stay afloat and keep up the façade that his lifestyle is natural and effortless.

The more you say a stereotype, repeat it, and live your life according to it, you breathe it into your world as a truth, and, unfortunately, your thoughts negatively influence permeable minds within earshot. Doing so, with great belief and relentless anger, results in your creation of a universe or society that will not achieve your desired results.

White men have thousands of kids out of wedlock from America to many of the countries in Asia. White men, more than any other race of men on the planet, are infamous for planting seeds across the globe. That's why we have so many different complexions and tones — from Thomas Jefferson and his peers to U.S. Soldiers fighting abroad and scruple-less others have done and continue to do what they want without recourse, and 100% of them never married the black and Asian women they had/have children with. An astonishing revelation to take note of is this: children made by white men and black women, who are reared alone by black women, are considered black children raised in a single-parent household. The number of black children fathered by absentee white men is very large, and this drastically tilts the scale against black men because it is perceived the aforementioned children, or any children born by black women, were fathered by black men because the child is classified as black. I, personally, know a white man that is single, but has fathered five children with a three black women. All five of those children are raised in a single-parent home, but none of them were made with a black man.

The amount of ammunition against white men continues with instances of white men committing domestic abuse, white men using drugs, white men committing homicide on their women and children, white men engaging in both blue-collar and white-collar crimes, and white men willing to taste the black women's fruit but unwilling to introduce her to his parents and friends. I choose to take the high road and not focus attention on their ills because this is about us. My point remains; the right black man is always the best man for a black woman.

As for white men having fathers teach them to hunt, fish, buy stocks, and provide for their families, more black men were brought up and still practice these activities. Simultaneously, many white men do not practice these activities. Everything mentioned, along with many other activities such as reading, skiing, carpentry, car mechanics, entrepreneurship, golf, construction, and others, are taught by different people in different regions according to interests, availability, and tradition. These activities are not owned, controlled, nor relegated to any one group or race.

There is something wrong with black women marrying white men and black men marrying white women if the relationship is based on unsubstantiated and frivolous stereotypes.

Do not be swayed by high-profile black celebrities and officials marrying white and Latino women. For every Kobe Bryant and Cuba Gooding Jr. there are multiple Denzel Washingtons, Jay-Zs, Will Smiths, Rodney Peetes, Judge Greg Mathis, Ice Cubes, Donovan McNabbs, etc. An optimistic eye sees beyond the tree and looks at the entire forest. The high-profile interracial couples are a minority compared to black couples.

As far as being disgusted with California men goes, keep in mind there are hundreds of thousands of macrocosms at your discretion within your own race outside of California. Set aside the 'ifs, ands, and buts,' and take a chance on building a relationship with men that are built for you. Do not be fearful, pessimistic, or hesitant.

Pardon me, but I am through with debating the topic. Let me talk with you — black man to black woman. Look, I know how you feel. I know your frustration with black men is overwhelming at times, but please keep in mind that we need you. We cannot do without you and the love, strength, and support you provide. For those of us that have our priorities in the wrong place and shun responsibility, the solution to get us on the right path is your complete encouragement. Without question, black women are the best "thing" on earth for black men. No one loves and can love a black woman the way a black man can. Let us create healthy black families that find reasons to stay together and build constructively instead of going to war with one another and tearing each other down. As a black man, I need you, we need you, and society needs us.

CHAPTER 16

Spousal Support

Okay, so Marlon let me have it. I respect everything he has to say. We can have a difference of opinion and still walk away as friends. I value Marlon's opinion, which is why I invited him to write something in the black man's defense, because not only is he educated, successful, articulate, and handsome, he's also married to a black woman! He isn't speaking as a male who's single, claiming to not be able to find a good woman, nor is he a black man turned off by black women. He celebrates us, supports us, and understands our frustrations when it comes to "waiting" for our suitor. He also doesn't have babies all over the country, so I find him to be a stand-up guy and an example to all black men.

With that said, I will go into the whole purpose of this chapter. When I first began writing this book during the Summer, 2007, I had no idea who Barack Obama was. More importantly, I had no idea who Michelle Obama was. From the first time I turned on my television and heard her speak so eloquently of her husband, I was in awe. She was amazing.

She was beautiful. She was smart, successful, dynamic, assertive, and geez, married to Him! Barack's public speaking was amazing in itself, but the two of them as a team, that was my idea of spousal support. She was not some brainless Hollywood Barbie Doll looking for photos ops or sitting there just to be pretty. She was so intelligent that her presence was instrumental in his winning not only the Democratic ticket, but the election, itself.

At the beginning of it all, I was slightly torn between Hillary and Barack for the nomination. However, after I heard Michelle speak, I knew who I would be voting for. So, if the President of the U.S., the most important man in America (*sorry Bill Cosby, I know you thought you were*) can find, meet, marry, and take on the world with a black woman at his side, then I think the men in my circle, who say they can't find us, are running out of excuses.

I put this whole book project on hold to support the election. I knew it would be a life-changing experience whether Barack Obama won or not. It was something I could be a part of. When I was nine years old, I was too young when Jesse Jackson ran. I was like, "why would a baseball player want to be President (confusing him with Reggie Jackson).

So now, we have Michelle as a role model to follow. We have an icon, in her own right, to look up to. It isn't because she wiggles her half-naked body across a stage to overly produced loud music, blinding lights, with pounds of fake hair and calls herself a diva. It is because she's showing black women all over the country, the world and on our planet that we don't have to settle for less. It also shows that when you find a good man, you can push him to be all that he can be. When he becomes the man he's supposed to be, if you are secure within yourself, you will reap the benefits. It's not about competition.

It's about spousal support. That is the type of love, relationship, success, and marriage we need as examples in our community.

Barack is not the only intelligent black man out there, although society would like to have us believe that he is. Michelle is not the only woman cut from that type of cloth, although the media constantly wants to make it appear as though she is. Barack and Michelle Obama are our leaders and if we operate within our potential, we may not be President and First Lady of the United States, but we can enjoy the same successes in our community, together. Wake up black man, we still need you.

CHAPTER 17

The Community Speaks

I am a blogger. I have been blogging about this topic for over a year so that I could get feedback from people who do not know me. I wanted to know how people felt about the subject of black women dating white men. I posted a thread on Tyra Banks' site and these are some of the things her followers had to say:

Reader – 'Hi Cicely J, and thank you so much for your reply to my post. I must apologize, because I do tend to take things literally. As much as I try not to be, I'm sensitive, and I feel racism pulling our nation apart.'

Cicely J: 'Don't apologize for having strong feelings about what our nation is going through and what you believe in. This is not just a problem that I and my single girlfriends are facing, it is a bigger issue that our nation is facing and no one wants to address it because everyone is trying to be so politically correct.

Reader – 'I am very glad to know there are intelligent people like you in the world who know that good qualities can be found in any race. Still, I believe the black community is often too hard on each other. How can a group of people ever be okay if they have no faith in each other?'

Cicely J: 'Actually I don't think we are hard enough. We need to place responsibility on individuals and hold people accountable. I will speak more specifically about black men because that is my initial topic. If men are to head the households and these black men are not equipped to do that because "we are being too hard on them" then we are going to continue to see a fleet of dysfunctional relationships, marriages, and children. Children become adults and have their own dysfunctions. Therefore, the cycle continues. I have faith. I believe in the black man. I trust that he can make it with the proper tools and right woman by his side, however, if I am never given the opportunity to support his dreams, desires, and goals, then I have to offer my support to someone else who is eager to wife me and create a family with me. That is what God intended. He didn't create Eve to be Adam's baby mama…Eve was his wife first…She supported everything he did in the Garden of Africa (Eden).'

Reader – 'Why not encourage good behavior instead of assuming the worst? The decay of morals is not exclusive to any one race, and it is not going to get better by blaming everyone else.'

Cicely J: 'I encourage and applaud good behavior but I am also not going to reward bad behavior and close my eyes to what is going on. I am not bashful nor am I shy and I refuse to pat the black man on the back and say "keep it up" when I don't think he is doing an excellent job. I am going to put him on blast and let him know what I think. Now I know some of us (women) are not all that together ourselves but it stems from what is happening to our men. Men were designed to lead. We were designed to   support, honor, obey, and follow. We can't follow these men if they are being punks, not getting an education, and fathering all of these children out of wedlock. From the dope dealer, to the NBA players, to the politicians, and the pastors, someone needs to let him know that he is not being a good example and he is not a man just because he has a penis. Everyone keeps referring to anatomy. That does not make you a man. It makes you male.'

Reader – 'We, all members of the human race need to address what happens to little children who are abused or neglected, and they grow up to be just as dysfunctional as the parents.'

Cicely J: 'I know all about them. I am a mentor and my mom has a group home. The bulk of the children are black males. I am doing my part but I am only one person. I don't just see the problem and talk about it; I am active in the communities. I go to the ghettos of Richmond and Oakland and show these youngstas a better way of life and what they can achieve if they break their father's cycle and the generational curses. I was raised in Suburbia. We were the only black family in my neighborhood, I went to private school and most of my friends were white but when I make it and am able to make a difference everything I do is for the children of the community my parents tried to keep me away from. I am not naïve about what is happening in the World. I know some mothers on welfare who have to apply for section 8 (subsidized housing) to take care of her fatherless children. This is not a community problem, this is a world problem. Black men, rich and poor need to come together and share the responsibility of rearing these children. That's what we did when we were in Africa. "It takes a village" is an old African saying and as long as we held true to that we were alright. Now we have the mentality, "it's me, my four and no more" and we have a generation of selfish bastards who are riding in Benz's, living high on the hog and his son doesn't have shoes that fit. I am not being hard enough, if you ask me.'

Reader –'This is where the real problems lie in any community. So, hopefully people will start to realize that how they raise their children has an impact on their entire lives, maybe then we would not have so many dead-beat parents in this world. Let's not forget a lot of women should be paying child support, too.

Cicely J: 'I'm glad you mentioned the women too. Some of us are enablers. We want the man to pay child support but then act stupid when he tries to see his children (for those men who actually want to be an active role). Sometimes it's easier for the man to walk away than stay there with the extra drama this woman is pushing at him. Everybody can't be together. If you have an unhealthy relationship then no, your child does not need to be in the middle of all that hatred. But take an active role. Don't bad mouth her because you two are not together, and stop expecting these women to perform as your wife when she is nothing more than the vessel to your illegitimate child(ren). If there is no ring, no vows, no marriage, I am not obligated to make you a ham sandwich or let you spend the night. So does that make me a B-I-T-C-H because I don't want to deal with a man's B.S. who is not even my husband? Damn child support, why does "the MAN" have to tell you to take care of your kids. Not only is he telling you. but he is taking your money before you even get it because he knows you are not going to pay otherwise. If you have kids, take care of them PERIOD!!!! If people had more respect and common sense child support would never even make it to the check.'

To my friend Art and any other black man of whom it applies:

While I enjoy reading what you write because you are quite eloquent, as I said before, I also notice that you are full of excuses. Men and women are different creatures; let's all agree on that first. The title *Men are from Mars and Women are from Venus* is just as much a very valid statement.

To the same degree black men are different from their white counterparts. No one said better; at least I didn't. I said different. More and more of our black men are choosing to be "whores" than to be the supportive husbands and fathers we need. Then when we (meaning successful/educated women) choose to date someone of another background or ethnicity, we are frowned upon.

Okay, you are an artist, and women love that. You are black with an ethnic appearance and most women into arts like that, as well, however you have self-proclaimed to everyone on Tyra's message board that you are a whore. You are proud of that label that you have given yourself. I don't judge anyone for what they do behind closed doors. I'm no angel, myself, but the design of the man was to SERVE one woman and vice versa. Why is it easier for us to find that chivalry in a man who is not black?

Black man we love you, but you won't love us back. We support you, but you are intimidated because we make more than you. We want to give you our heart, body, and soul, but you are constantly putting us in the bed with everyone else you are sleeping with. I'm sorry black man, but I'm selfish. I don't want the lovin' that is supposed to be only mine shared with half of the single, females in the lonely hearts' club. I like the fact that they are attracted to you. I have something worth holding on to, but I'm saddened that you don't look at me the same way. To you, I'm not indispensable, but replaceable because the ratio is so imbalanced.

You are not afraid to lose me because someone else is always ready to step in and take my place. This relationship is not about walking on egg shells and making sure that I never upset you. If you love me and spend any amount of time with me, the day is going to come that I will upset you. I want you (black man) to understand that this life is not about getting everything you want… it's about being there to supply the need.

We need a community of black leaders. We need more black owned businesses. We need black men who are going to stand for what is right and check their homey when he's out of pocket. Don't give him dap when he shows up with his sexy girlfriend while his wife, who just had a baby, is at home. We need more black male professors who are married to black women. We need to support black restaurants in our neighborhoods. We need more fathers to go up to the schools and meet their children's teachers.

Black man, we need you to love us because although the cosmetic companies are creating everything to look like us, they are still telling us we are not good enough; we are not pretty enough; we are not light enough; we are not skinny enough, etc. If our own men don't accept us and throw white women in our faces because they think they're better to be with, then what are we supposed to do? I'll tell you what… we find one black woman with a big mouth and a brain (me) to write a book about how trifling y'all are, and we have decided to date "others" because we are tired of waiting. Then I get all the hate-mail and the name calling and, frankly, I don't care. I'll stand on the front line of the battlefield, if that's what it takes. But I'll tell you another thing, you poetic black man; you are not going to piss on us and say you're spraying us with perfume; at least, not anymore.

If you can't handle that responsibility, then please don't sleep with me and make me want to be with you. All the black woman wants to do is love the RIGHT black man.

Reader - 'What's the big deal? Anybody should be able to date anybody, whomever they prefer.'

What Black women, who date white men, quickly come to find out is that: 1) the white man is not perfect; 2) He's a man and he brings his own set of problems. He may not bring the same problems as the black man, but   human is human. He has his own bag. And the same is true of Black men who date whites or Asians or Hispanic women. The other race is not a panacea, they are just variety; an additional pool. At the end of the day, the object is to make a soul connection with a decent human being. There is nothing wrong with people of different ages, races, cultures or backgroundconsorting.

What I've learned as a black man is that women of other races like us (the black man) for the exact same reason the black woman likes us. Racism, smay-shism. Women, black or otherwise, like us. And they are brazen about competing for our affections. Nah, sister, free love shouldn't bother anybody. But something is the matter with you, if you are condescending, and are one of those successful, self-righteous black chicks for whom the black man is not good enough. If, in advocating for the other man you are tearing down & bad mouthing the black man (not saying you are her), then you might be a disgrace.

You know that chick who NEVER dates black men. And then when asked why, she ticks off a long list of tired generalizations that reduce the black man down to a caricature; a character. As if God left out something essential in us. Naw, it ain't all about cock. Other women like our mind, soul, swag & sense of humor.

'Well, if you are one of those "the Black man ain't s#!t," sisters, then if the shoe fits, put it on and wear it; because, there is a decent, sincere, single black man out there who is on your level. I don't buy that black man as endangered species stuff; brothers out here hoping a queen will fall into his lap.'

Cicely J: I agree with you, wholeheartedly. My ultimate point is that, instead of sitting at home alone and not having the family you want because there is an evident and apparent shortage of good black men out there, consider dating "other" as we have seen our black men do for years now.

I am from California and interracial dating is accepted and celebrated out here, more so, than other more rural areas. I'm not exclusive to any ethnic group and I will marry a white man   before I spend the rest of my life by myself simply because I can't seem to find a decent, educated, good credit-having black man without three baby mama's and a prison record. I'm just saying.

This book has gone way more into depth about the serious problems and the numbers of black men in prison vs. black men in college, as well as the number of black men with degrees and the number of college dropouts. This is not a bash-all-brothers book. It's about what is happening in our communities and how our African American heritage is being wiped out.

You seem intelligent enough to know that it IS a big deal that there are more mixed kids at my son's school, my son included, than there are white or black. Is it me or do we only see successful black men in the form of sports players, rappers, or other entertainers? Where are the doctors, lawyers, politicians (other than Obama), engineers, chemists, etc? They are married to white women. Hey, we'll settle for the Alhambra postal worker or cable man, but he's married to a Mexican. We're no longer the black man's first choice, so tit for tat; neither is he, anymore.

I like the black man's swag, too. Unfortunately, so do a hundred other women, so he has no reason or motivation to be faithful to me.

I don't want to be the damn Queen. Princesses have less responsibility and I have been doing this by myself, "<u>way</u>" too long. By the way, my shoe size is 8-1/2 and it fits well.'

Reader – 'You are right. You are wrong. Anybody who is self-aware knows what his strengths are and what his weaknesses are. And   relationships don't work in reality like they do in the SELF HELP BOOKS. Things are almost always way messier than the ideal. In relationships there is something like "market forces" at play. The law of supply & demand works in relationships. So, a good guy (or good girl), for that matter, knows that demand is high & supply is low. What they have is a valuable commodity, and they know who wants it or finds the commodity valuable. Thus, they know they have the option to trawl the waters to pick & choose. They don't have to settle. People "chase" goodness. Being "good" means that you have the power to initiate desire, and initiate the chase. Everybody who's ever been pursued knows who they want to catch them. When the ideal person is on the hunt, you don't make a great effort to elude them. You allow yourself to be trapped. I don't think the numbers of available partners are as significant as the qualities of the pursuer. Self-aware men know if they are good and they may use their goods to mislead, tantalize, tease and bag girls. But a person who does that is probably not good as he looks, and is greasy. Players, deceivers and con men travel this route.'

Reader - But let's be real too. A REAL MAN cannot & will not resist a real woman when she puts it in his face. If IT is good, and IT is real. He will get in his lane and run it straight. He won't run from responsibility, he will volunteer to take up some of the woman's burdens & put them on his back. He'll do anything and everything to ingratiate himself for the right one. Those are boys & users who view women as stepping stones and resources to drain. But a dude who values healthy relationships ain't playing the game like that. Before y'all lay down, y'all better understand the character of a man. Don't let the deep voice fool you. If you get burned by a guy who bones you, gets up, wipes his di@k on the curtains and leaves, that's your fault.'

Cicely J: Some points you make, I am 100% behind you on them. I guess great minds think alike, sometimes. Then you say something so to the left it, throws me off. Men are not just blatant dogs like that. If so, they would never be able to victimize intelligent women like myself. I agree you have to make the man work for it but, at the same time, you can't play TOO hard to get and never let him catch you. He will lose focus and start chasing someone else.

But some of these men have mastered allowing us to fall in love with him over time. If I am in love with a man there is nothing he can ask me to do that I wouldn't go out of my way and break my back to make sure it happens. That's what a woman in love will do... any woman. And men know this so they put in the time, make us fall in love, and then the real him surfaces. Life is real, but love has become game. We were on the losing end, at first, but we are becoming stronger and wiser to the game. Now these doggish men are becoming our "practice piece" and we are longing for the "good guy," whether he is black or white. You can't treat me wrong unless I allow you to, and I don't care what you do if I am not in love with you. Do whatever you want because I am the confident one who knows that it is HIS loss and not mine.

Now if you give it up and have not established any type of commitment or relationship with this man, then your fault if he bounces, leaves his number on the table, and you never hear from him again. Be a woman and be prepared for it, if it happens. But, if we have put in time with each other and I am still not getting what I thought I was bargaining for, then it's time to reflect, readjust, and reassign. In other words if I can be met halfway, I am not wasting my time.'

In conclusion, trust me, when I say that I did not intend to create friction when I decided to write this book and post a thread online about it. I want to make a few points and this is directed to everyone.

I don't think brothers should shrug their shoulders and say "Oh well, love who you want to love," when you see a black woman with a white man. Sometimes there are valid reasons why she is dating or married to that white man. Brothers need to take an active part in identifying what the problem is and try fixing it. We all have our   shortcomings but, if I express how I feel and what you are doing to me, don't get defensive. Correct it. Don't turn around and list all of my faults, like we're going tit for tat.

In the 21st Century, society still has a problem seeing interracial couples; specifically, black & white. Like I said before, I love black men, I date black men, and one day I plan to be married to a black man. However, I keep my options open. I also encourage other black women to do the same.

That is the point I'm trying to make. Don't sit back my sisters and wait for your Prince Charming. He's not going to knock on your door and whisk you away. Broaden your horizons, expand your interests, get a passport, travel abroad and let love find you; in whatever shape, color, or persona that may be. There's no need or intent for anger.

Let's all self reflect. Black women have a list of things about black men and black men have a list of things about black women. We have to live on the planet together, so we must respect each other and be allowed to voice our opinions without being judged or misunderstood. If I'm not clear in my dissertation, then put me on notice so I can make sure my communication is plain and concise.

I have aimed for excellence in every aspect of my life and will accept nothing less from my partner and potential life's mate. He can be black, white, purple, green, or orange. All I ask is that I am respected and loved. That is what we all should want. By no means, am I saying that a brother should approach a sister he sees in an interracial relationship and question her motives. I'm saying that there is a reason why we are seeing it so much.

Black men are not eager to settle down and get married anymore. Black men are known to be promiscuous and cheat on their girlfriends, wives, and baby mamas. More black women are going to college and getting an education than our black men. More black women are working their way up the corporate ladder and, therefore, our pickings are getting scarcer than hen's teeth.

I went to lunch a couple of days ago with a girlfriend of mine. Of course, we were the only two black people at the restaurant. It was a beautiful sunny day, so we decided to sit out on the patio. Men were gawking and staring at us the entire time we were there. The only black person I saw walk past the restaurant was a cute thin black man who switched harder that Naomi Campbell on the catwalk.

I get frustrated, sometimes. We take these corporate power lunches and I don't see a black man with a suit on at any of the tables. It's me against the world.

Where are the black men who are going to get on the front line with the black woman? Where is the black man who is going to work with me and be supportive of my dreams and my drive and not just be in it for the ride? Where is the black man who is going to allow me to support him and be his rock and not feel intimidated or weak because he needs me?

I live in the Bay Area and work in San Francisco. He's not here. I stopped looking. I stopped expecting it, because I don't see him anywhere. I go across the bridge to Oakland and all I see are saggin' pants, braids, and gold and diamond fronts and grills. He cannot come to the corporate dinner party with me and my colleagues.

So black man, give us something to look at, something worth fighting for, and something to hold on to. Don't just sit back and watch YOUR WOMEN be swept away by another race.

Who understands us better than you? Who can maintain and sustain us better than you? Who has been through the same struggle we go through, everyday, proving our worth, other than you? No one. Not one other race has gone through what we have and, yet, we can't be with each other and have each other's back.

I will say it again and keep saying it; I LOVE BLACK MEN... my book will not denounce that even once. However, being the type of black woman I am, it's hard to find what I *need* in a black man; one who wants a family, wants to be married, has an entrepreneurial mind and background; one who is not intimidated by my education, my ambition, my drive, and me owning my own businesses; one who wants the finer things in life and knows how to go get it; someone who can encourage me and give me business advice.

I don't know it all but I want a man I can learn something from; someone who is tall in stature, but humble in spirit; not a flashy, materialistic man who wants to be seen, but a hardworking man who wants to be comfortable with me; someone who will laugh at my jokes and hug me when I want to cry; someone who will rub my feet when I have had a long day and will sit back and let me rub his when I know my man is tired.

I want someone who enjoys eating my food (yes, I can cook) and he will cook for me when I want to be spoiled and catered to, once in a while; a man who will hold my purse for me when I go into the dressing room to try something on; a man who will open the door for me and walk on the outside of the sidewalk; a man who will go to church with me (not every Sunday but more than just on Christmas and Easter); and a man who will go to a comedy club with me.

I want someone with a balance, a sense of humor, a goal, and a plan. That is the man I will love, honor, and obey. I can submit myself to a man like that. But in my prerequisite, (which means "search" for you non-literary scholars) I find more and more, unfortunately, who may not be black. My first choice is a black man, but my final choice is to not live this great life alone. Am I asking for too much?

Look out for my next book entitled, "The Skin I'm In," as I delve deeply into the life of a successful black man who comes to a crossroads in his life when his wife finds pictures of him with his ex-boyfriend.

www.ingramcontent.com/pod-product-compliance
Lightning Source LLC
Chambersburg PA
CBHW060423260626
47161CB00005B/1758